Doris Lessing

*L*ondon
*O*bserved

STORIES AND SKETCHES

HarperCollins*Publishers*

HarperCollins*Publishers*
77–85 Fulham Palace Road,
Hammersmith, London W6 8JB

Published by HarperCollins*Publishers* 1992
9 8 7 6 5 4 3 2 1

Some of these stories first appeared in the following
publications: *The Observer Magazine, The Independent
Magazine, Fiction Magazine, London Magazine, Hampstead &
Highgate Express, Irish Times, Mississippi Valley Review,
Icarus, Antaeus* and *The New Yorker*

The Author asserts the moral right to
be identified as the author of this work

A catalogue record for this book
is available from the British Library

ISBN 0 00 223935 3

Set in Palatino

Printed in Great Britain by
HarperCollinsManufacturing Glasgow

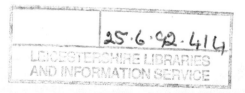

Contents

Debbie
and
Julie

The fat girl in the sky-blue coat again took herself to the mirror. She could not keep away from it. Why did the others not comment on her scarlet cheeks, just like when she got measles, and the way her hair was stuck down with sweat? But they didn't notice her; she thought they did not see her. This was because of Debbie who protected her, so they got nothing out of noticing her.

She knew it was cold outside, for she had opened a window to check. Inside this flat it was, she believed, warm, but the heating in the block was erratic, particularly in bad weather, and then the electric fires were brought out and Debbie swore and complained and said she was going to move. But Julie knew Debbie would not move. She could not: she had fought for this flat to be hers, and people (men) from everywhere – 'from all over the world', as Julie would proudly say to herself, knew Debbie was here. And besides, Julie was going to need to think of Debbie here, when she herself got home: remember the bright rackety place where people came and went, some of them frightening, but none threatening her, Julie, because Debbie looked after her.

She was so wet she was afraid she would start squelching.

What if the wet came through the coat? Back she went to the bathroom and took off the coat. The dress – Debbie's, like the once smart coat – was now orange instead of yellow, because it was soaked. Julie knew there would be a lot of water at some point, because the paperback Debbie had bought her said so, but she didn't know if she was simply sweating. In the book everything was so tidy and regular, and she had checked the stages she must expect a dozen times. But now she stood surrounded by jars of bath salts and lotions on the shelf that went all around the bathroom, her feet wide apart on a fluffy rug like a terrier's coat, and felt cold water springing from her forehead, hot water running down her legs. She seemed to have pains everywhere, but could not match what she felt with the book.

On went the blue coat again. It was luckily still loose on her, for Debbie was a big girl, and she was small. Back she went to the long mirror in Debbie's room, and what she saw on her face, a look of distracted pain, made her decide it was time to leave. She longed for Debbie, who might after all just turn up. She could not bear to go without seeing her . . . *she had promised!* But she had to, now, at once, and she wrote on a piece of paper she had kept ready just in case. 'I am going now. Thanks for everything. Thank you, thank you, thank you. All my love, Julie.' Then her home address. She stuck this letter in a sober white envelope into the frame of Debbie's mirror and went into the living room, where a lot of people were lolling about watching the TV. No, not really a lot, four people crammed the little room. No one even looked at her. Then the man she was afraid of, and who had tried to 'get' her, took in the fact that she stood there, enormous and smiling foolishly in her blue coat, and gave her the look she always got from him, which said he didn't know why Debbie bothered with her but didn't care. He was a sharp clever man, handsome she supposed, in a flashy Arab way. He was from Lebanon, and she must make allowances because there was a war there. Sitting beside him on the sofa was the girl who took the drugs around for him. She was smart and clever, like him, but blonde and shiny, and she looked like a model for cheap clothes. A model was what she said she was, but Julie knew she wasn't. And there were two girls Julie had never seen before, and she supposed they were innocents, as she had been. They looked all giggly and anxious to please, and they were waiting. For Debbie?

Julie went quietly through the room to the landing outside and stood watching for the lift. She checked her carrier bag, ready for a month now, stuffed under her bed. In it was a torch, pieces of string wrapped in a piece of plastic, two pairs of knickers, a cardigan, a thick towel with an old blouse of Debbie's cut open to lie flat inside it and be soft and satiny, and some sanitary pads. The pads were Debbie's. She bled a lot each month. The lift came but Julie had gone back into the flat, full of trouble and worry. She felt ill-prepared, she did not have enough of something, but what could it be? The way she felt told her nothing, except that what was going to happen would be uncontrollable, and until today she had felt in control, and even confident. From shelves in the bathroom she took, almost at random, some guest towels and stuffed them into the carrier. She told herself she was stealing from Debbie, but knew Debbie wouldn't mind. She never did, would say only, 'Just take it, love, if you want it.' Then she might laugh and say, 'Take what you want and *don't* pay for it!' Which was her motto in life, she claimed on every possible occasion. Julie knew better. Debbie could say this as much as she liked, but what she, Julie, had learned from Debbie was, simply, this: what things cost, the value of everything, and of people, of what you did for them, and what they did for you. When she had first come into this flat, brought by Debbie, who had seen her standing like a dummy on the platform at Waterloo at midnight on that first evening she arrived by herself in London, she had been as green as . . . those girls next door, waiting, but not knowing what for. She had been innocent and silly, and what that all boiled down to was that she hadn't known the price of anything. She hadn't known what had to be paid. This was what she had learned from Debbie, even though Debbie had never allowed her to pay for anything, ever.

From the moment she had been seen on the platform five months ago on a muggy, drizzly August evening, she had been learning how ignorant she was. For one thing, it was not only Debbie who had seen her; a lot of other people on the lookout in various parts of the station would have moved in on her like sharks if Debbie hadn't got to her first. Some of these people were baddies and some were goodies, but the kind ones would have sent her straight home.

For the second time she went through the living room and no one looked at her. The Lebanese was smiling and talking in an elder-brotherly way to the new girls. Well, they had better watch out for themselves.

For the second time she waited for the lift. She seemed quite wrenched with pain. Was it worse? Yes, it was.

In the bitter black street that shone with lights from the lamps and the speeding cars she hauled herself on to a bus. Three stops, and by the time she reached where she wanted, she knew she had cut it too fine. She got off in a sleet shower under a street lamp and saw her blue coat turning dark with wet. Now she was far from being too hot, she was ready to shiver and shake, but could not decide if this was panic. Everything she had planned had seemed so easy, one thing after another, but she had not foreseen that she would stand at a bus stop, afraid to leave the light there, not knowing what the sensations were that wrenched her body. Was she hot? Cold? Nauseous? Hungry? A good thing the weather was so bad, no one was about. She walked boldly through the sleet and turned into a dark and narrow alley where she hurried, because it smelled bad and scared her, then out into a yard full of builders' rubbish and rusty skips. There was a derelict shed at one end. This shed was where she was going, where she had been only three days before to make sure it was still there, had not been pulled down, and that she could get in the door. But now something she had not foreseen. A large dog stood in the door, a great black threatening beast, and it was growling. She could see the gleam of its teeth and eyes. But she knew she had to get into the shed, and quickly. Again water poured hotly down her legs. Her head was swimming. Hot knives carved her back. She found a half brick and flung it at the wall near the dog, who disappeared into the shed growling. This was awful . . . Julie went into the shed, shut the door behind her, with difficulty because it dragged on broken hinges, and switched on the torch. The dog stood against a wall looking at her, but now she could see it would not hurt her. Its tail was sweeping about in the dirt, and it was so thin she could see its ribs under the dirty black shabby fur. Its eyes were bright and frantic. It wanted her to be good to it. She said, 'It's all right, it's only me,' and went to the corner of the shed away from the dog, where she had spread a folded blanket. The blanket was there, but the dog had been lying on it. She turned the blanket so the clean part inside was on the top. Now, having reached her refuge, she didn't know what to do. She took off her soaking knickers. She put the carrier bag close to the blanket. Afraid someone might see the gleam of light, she switched off the torch, first making sure she knew where it was. She could hear the dog breathing, and the flap-flap of its tail. It was lying down, not far from her. She could smell the wet doggy smell, and she was grateful for that, pleased the dog was there. Now she was in no doubt she had got here just in time, because her whole body was hot and fierce with pain, and she wanted to cry out, but knew she must not. She was groaning, though, and she heard herself: 'Debbie, Debbie, Debbie . . .' All those months Debbie had said, 'Don't worry about anything, when the time comes I'll see everything's all right.' But Debbie had gone off with the new man to Paris, saying she would be back in a week, but had rung from New York to say, 'How are you, honey? I'll be back at the weekend.' That was three weeks ago. The 'honey' had told Julie this man was different from the others, not only because he was an American: Debbie had never called her anything but Julie, wouldn't have dreamed of changing her behaviour for any man, but this 'honey' had not been for Julie, but for the man who was listening. 'I don't blame her,' Julie was muttering now. 'She always said she wanted just one man, not Tom and Dick and Harry.' But while Julie was making herself think, I don't blame her, she was groaning, 'Oh, Debbie, Debbie, why did you leave me?'

Debbie had left her to cope on her own, after providing everything from shelter and food and visits to a doctor, to the clothes and the bright blue coat that had hidden her so well no one had known. Debbie and she joked how little people noticed about other people. 'You'd better watch your diet,' the Lebanese had said. 'Don't you let her' – meaning Debbie – 'stuff you with food all the time.'

Julie was on all fours on the blanket, her head between her arms, her fists clenched tight, and she was crying. The pain was awful, but that wasn't the worst of it. She felt so alone, so lonely. It occurred to her that having her

bottom up in the air was probably not the right thing. She
squatted, her back against a cold brick wall, and went on
sweating and moaning. She could hear the dog whining,
in sympathy, she thought. Water, or was it blood, poured
out. She was afraid to switch on the torch to see. She felt
the dog sniff at her face and neck, but it went off again.
She could see absolutely nothing, it was so dark. Then
she felt a rush, as if her insides were pouring out, and
she thought, Why didn't the book say there would be
all this water all the time? Then she thought, But that's
the baby, and put her hand down and under her on the
blanket was a wet slippery lump. She felt for the torch
and switched it on. The baby was greyish and bloody
and its mouth was opening and shutting. Now she was
in a panic. Before, she had decided she must wait before
cutting the cord, because the paperback said there was no
hurry, but she was desperate to get the cord cut, in case
the baby died. She found where the cord came out of the
baby, a thick twisted rope of flesh, full of life, hot and
pulsing in her hand. She found the scissors. She found
the string. She cut the birth cord with the scissors, and
trembled with fear. Blood everywhere, and the dog had
come close and was sitting so near she could touch it. Its
eyes were saying, Please, please . . . It was gulping and
licking its lips, because of all the blood, when it was so
hungry.

'You wait a bit,' she said to the poor dog. Now she tied
the cord up with the string that had boiled a long time in
the saucepan. She was worrying because she was getting
something wrong, but couldn't remember what it was. As
for boiling the string, what sense did that make, when you
saw the filth in this shed. Tramps had used it. The dog . . .
other dogs too, probably. For all she knew, other girls had
given birth in it. Most sheds were garden sheds, and full
of plants in pots, and locked up. She knew, because she

had checked so many. Not many places where a girl could give birth to a baby in peace and quiet – or a stray dog find a dry place out of the rain . . . She was getting giggly and silly, she could feel herself losing control. Meanwhile the baby was lying in a pool of bloody water and was mouthing and pulling its face about, and she ought to be doing something. Surely it ought to be crying? It was so slippery. The paperback didn't say anything about the baby being greasy and wet and so slippery she would be afraid to lift it. She pulled out the bundle of towel from the carrier and laid it flat, with the soft pink satin of Debbie's blouse smooth on top. She used both hands to pick the baby up round its middle and felt it squirm, probably because her hands were so cold. Its wriggling strength, its warmth, the life she could feel beating there, astonished and pleased her. Unexpectedly she was full of pleasure and pride. The baby's perfectly all right, she thought, looking in the torchlight at hands, feet . . . what else should she look for? Oh, yes, it was a girl. Was it deformed? The baby had an enormous cunt, a long wrinkled slit. Was that normal? Why didn't the book say?

She folded the baby firmly into the towel, with the bottom of the towel well tucked in over its feet, and only its face showing. Then she picked it up. It began to roar in short angry spasms. And now the panic began again. She had not thought the baby would cry so loudly . . . someone would come . . . what should she do . . . but she couldn't leave the shed because there was a thing called the afterbirth. As she thought this, there was another wet rush, all down her legs, and out plopped a mass of something that looked like liver with the end of the thick red cord coming out of it.

And now she knew what to do. She raised herself from the squatting position, clutching the baby with one arm and using the other hand to push herself up from the floor. She stood shakily by the bloody mess and moved away a few paces with the baby held high up and close against her. At once the dog crawled forward, giving her a desperate look that said, Don't get in my way. It ate up the afterbirth in quick gulps. It hopefully licked the bloody blanket, and briefly lifted its muzzle to look at her, wagging its long dirty tail. Then it went back to its place and sat with its back to the wall, watching. Meanwhile the baby let out short angry cries and kicked hard in its cocoon of towel. Julie thought, Should I just leave the baby here and run for it? No, the dog . . . But as she thought this, the baby stopped and lay quietly looking at her. Well, she wasn't going to look back, she wasn't going to love it.

She had to leave here, and she was a swamp of blood, water, God only knew what.

She took a cautious look. Blood trickled down her legs. And she had actually believed a tampon or two would be enough! She laid the baby down on a clean place on the blanket, keeping an eye on the dog. Its eyes gleamed in the torchlight. She put on a pair of clean knickers and packed in sanitary towels. She tried to tie the guest towels around her waist to make an extra pad, but they were too stiff. Now she picked up the baby, which was just like a papoose and looking around with its blurry little eyes. She took up the carrier bag and then the torch. She said to the dog, 'Poor dog, I'm sorry,' and went out, making sure the door was open for the dog. She switched off the torch, though the ground was rough and had bricks and bits of wood lying about. She could just see: there were lights in windows high up across the street. The sleet still blew down. She was already shivering. And the baby only had the towel around it . . . She put the bundle of baby under the flap of the now loose coat and went quickly across the uneven ground to the alley, and then through the bad-smelling place and then along the pavement to a telephone box she had made sure would be conveniently close when she was looking for the shed or somewhere safe. There was no one near the telephone box, no one anywhere around. She put the baby down on the floor and walked towards the brilliant lights of the pub at the corner. She did not look back. The pub was crammed and hot and noisy. Now what she was afraid of was that she might smell so strongly of blood someone would notice. She could hardly make her way to the toilet. There she removed her knickers with the pads of sanitary towels, which were already soaked. She used one of the guest towels to wash herself down. She went on soaking the towel in hot water and wringing it out, then wiping herself, watching how the blood at once began trickling on to the clean white skin of her inner thighs. But she could not stay there for ever, washing. She rubbed the same towel, wrung out in hot water, over her sticky head. She combed her hair flat. Well, it wouldn't stay flat for long: being naturally curly it would spring back into its own shape soon. Debbie said it was sweet, like a little girl. She filled her knickers with new pads, put the bloody pads into the container, and went out into the pub. Now there was music from the jukebox, pounding away, and the beat went straight through her, vibrating and making her feel sick. She wanted badly to get away from the music, but she bought a shandy, reaching over the shoulders of men arguing about football to get it. Unremarked, she went to stand near a small window that overlooked the telephone box. She could see the bundle, a small pathetic thing, like folded newspapers or a dropped jersey, on the floor of the box. She had first found the shed, then looked for the telephone box, and then hoped there would be a window somewhere close by, and there was.

She stood by the window for only five minutes or so. Then she saw a young man and a girl go into the telephone box. Through window glass streaked again with sleet, she saw the girl pick up the bundle from the floor, while the young man telephoned. She ought to leave . . . she ought not to stand here . . . but she stayed, watching, while the noise of the pub beat around her. The ambulance came in no time. Two ambulance men. The girl came out of the telephone box with the bundle, and the young man was behind her. The ambulance men took the bundle, first one, then the other, then handed it back to the girl, who got into the ambulance. The young man stood on the pavement, and the girl inside waved to him, and he got in to go with them. So the baby was safe. It was done. She had done it. As she went out into the sleety rain she saw the ambulance lights vanish, and her heart plunged into loss and became empty and bitter, in the way she had been determined would not happen. 'Debbie,' she whispered, the tears running. 'Where are you, Debbie?' Not necessarily New York. Or even the States. Canada . . . Mexico . . . the Costa Brava . . . South America . . . The people coming and going in Debbie's flat were always off somewhere, or just back. Rio . . . San Francisco, you name it. And Debbie had said to her, 'One day it will be your turn.' But now it was Debbie's turn. Why should she ever come back? She wanted to have 'just one regular customer'. Once she had said, by mistake, 'just one man'. Julie had heard this, but did not comment. Debbie could be as hard and as jokey as she liked, but she couldn't fool Julie, who knew she was the only person who really understood Debbie.

Now Julie was walking to the Underground, as fast as she could. Her legs were shaky, but she felt all right. All she wanted was to get home. It had been impossible to go home, or even think too much about home where her father (she was sure) would simply throw her out. But now, it was only a question of a few stops on the

Underground, and then the train. At the most, an hour and a half.

The Underground train was full of people. They had had a meal after work, or been in a pub. Like Julie! She kept looking at all those faces and thinking, What would you say if you knew? At Waterloo she sat on a bench near an old man with a drinker's face, a tramp. She gave him a pound, but she was thinking of the dog. She did not have to wait long for a train. It was not full. Surely she ought to be tired, or sick or something? Most of all she was hungry. A great plate of steak and eggs, that was what she needed. And Debbie there too, eating opposite her.

A plump fresh-faced girl in a damp sky-blue coat sat upright among the other home-goers, holding a carrier bag that had on it, written red on black, SUSIE'S STYLES! Her eyes shone. Her young fresh fair hair curled all over her head. She vibrated with confidence, with secrets.

At the station she had to decide between a bus and walking home. Not the bus: on it there'd almost certainly be someone she knew, and perhaps even from her school. She didn't want to be looked at yet. The sleet was now a chilly blowy rain, with the sting of ice in it, but it wasn't bad, more of an occasional sharp pattering coming into her face and invigorating her. But she was going to arrive home all wet and pathetic, not at all as she had planned.

When she turned into her street, lights showed behind the curtains in all the windows. No one was out. What was she going to do about that coat, wet through, and, worse, hanging on her? Her mother would notice all that space under the coat and wonder. Three doors from home she glanced around to make sure no one was watching, and stripped off the coat in one fast movement and dropped it into a dustbin. Even in this half dark, lit with dull gleams from a window, she could see blood-stains on the lining. And her dress? The yellow dress was limp and grubby, but the cardigan came down low and hid most of it. This was going to be the dangerous part, all right, and only luck would get her through it. She ran up the steps and rang the bell, smiling, while she clutched the carrier bag so it could hide her front, which was still squashy and fat where the baby had been.

Heavy steps. Her father. The door opened slowly while he fumbled at locks, and she kept the smile going, and her heart beat, and then he stood in front of her large and black with the light behind him, so that her heart went small and weak . . . but then he turned so she could see his face and she thought, That can't be him, that can't be my *father* – for he had shrunk and become grey and ordinary, and . . . *what on earth had she been afraid of?* She could just hear what Debbie would say about him! Why, he was nothing at all. He called out in a sharp barking voice, 'Anne, Anne, she's here.' He was a man waiting for his wife to take command, crying as he went stumbling down the hall. Julie's mother came fast towards her. She was already crying, and that meant she could not see anything much. She put her arms around Julie and sobbed and said, 'Oh, Julie, Julie, why didn't you . . . ? But come in, why, you're soaked.' And she pushed and pulled Julie towards, and then into, the living room, where the old man (which is how Julie was seeing him with her new eyes) sat bowed in his chair, tears running down his face.

'She's all right, Len,' said Anne, Julie's mother. She let go of her daughter and sat upright in her chair, knees together, feet together, dabbing her cheeks under her eyes, and stared at Len with a look that said, There, I told you so.

'Get her a cup of tea, Anne,' said Len. And then, to Julie, but without looking at her, looking at his wife in a heavy awful way that told Julie how full of calamity had been their discussions about her, 'Sit down, we aren't going to eat you.'

Julie sat on the edge of a chair, but gingerly, because it hurt. It was as if she had been anaesthetized by urgency, but now she was safe, pains and soreness could make themselves felt. She watched her parents weep, their bitter faces full of loss. She saw how they sat, each in a chair well apart from the other, not comforting each other, or holding her, or wanting to hold each other, or to hold her.

'Oh, Julie,' said her mother, 'oh, *Julie.*'

'Mum, can I have a sandwich?'

'Of course you can. We've had our supper. I'll just . . .'

Julie smiled, she could not help it, and it was a sour little smile. She knew that what had been on those plates was exactly calculated, not a pea or a bit of potato left over. The next proper meal (lunch, tomorrow) would already be on a plate ready to cook, with a plastic film over it, in the fridge. Her mother went off to the kitchen, to work out how to feed Julie, and now Julie was alone with her father, and that wasn't good.

'You mustn't think we are going to ask you awkward questions,' said her father, still not looking at her, and Julie knew that her mother had said, 'We mustn't ask her any awkward questions. We must wait for her to tell us.'

You bloody well ought to ask some questions, Julie was thinking, noting that already the raucous angry irritation her parents always made her feel was back, and strong. And, at the moment, dangerous.

But they had expected her to come back, then? For she had been making things easier for herself by saying, They won't care I'm not there! They probably won't even notice! Now she could see how much they had been grieving for her. How was she going to get herself out of here up to the bathroom? If she could just have a bath! At this point her mother came back with a cup of tea. Julie took it, drank it down at once, though it was too hot, and handed the cup back. She saw her mother had realized she meant it: she needed to eat, was hungry, could drink six cups of tea one after another. 'Would you mind if I had a bath, Mum? I won't take a minute. I fell and the street was all slippery. It was sleeting.'

She had already got herself to the door, clutching the carrier in front of her.

'You didn't hurt yourself?' enquired her father.

'No, I only slipped, I got all muddy.'

'You run along and have a bath, girl,' said her mother. 'It'll give me time to boil an egg for sandwiches.'

Julie ran upstairs. Quick, quick, she mustn't make a big thing of this bath, mustn't stay in it. Her bedroom was just so, all pretty and pink, and her big panda sat on her pillow. She flung off her clothes and waves of a nasty sour smell came up at her. She stuffed them all into the carrier and grabbed from the cupboard her pink-flowered dressing gown. What would Debbie have to say about that? she wondered, and wanted to laugh, thinking of Debbie here, sprawling on her bed with the panda. She found childish pyjamas stuffed into the back of a drawer. What was she going to do for padding? Her knickers showed patches of blood and that meant the pads hadn't been enough. She found some old panties and went into the bathroom with them. The bath filled quickly and there were waves of steam. Careful, she didn't want to faint, and her head was light. She got in and submerged her head. Quick, quick . . . She soaped and rubbed, getting rid of the birth, the dirty shed, the damp dog smell, the blood, all that blood. It was still welling gently out of her, not much but enough to make her careful when she dried herself on the fluffy pink towels her mother changed three times a week. She put on her knickers and packed them with old panties. On went the pyjamas, the pink dressing gown. She combed her hair.

There. It was all gone. Her breasts, she knew from the book, would have milk, but she would put on a tight bra and fill it with cotton wool. She would manage. In this house, her home, they did not see each other naked. Her mother hadn't come in for years when she was having a bath, and she always knocked on the bedroom door. In Debbie's flat people ran about naked or half dressed and Debbie might answer the door in her satin camiknickers, those great breasts of hers lolling about. Debbie often came in when Julie was in the bath to sit on the loo and chat . . . Tears filled Julie's eyes. Oh, no, she certainly must not cry.

She stuffed the bag with the bloody pads and her dirty clothes in it under her bed, well to the back. She would get rid of it all very early in the morning before her parents woke, which they would, at seven o'clock.

She went down the stairs, a good little girl washed and brushed, ready for the night.

In the living room her parents were silent and apart in their two well separated chairs. They had been crying again. Her father was relieved at what he saw when he cautiously took a look at her (as if it had been too painful to see her before), and he said, 'It's good to have you home, Julie.' His voice broke.

Her mother said, 'I've made you some nice sandwiches.'

Four thin slices of white bread had been made into two sandwiches and cut diagonally across, the yellow of the egg prettily showing, with sprigs of parsley disposed here and there. Hunger sprang in Julie like a tiger, and she ate ravenously, watching her mother's pitying, embarrassed face. Why, she thinks I've been short of food! Well, that's a good thing, it'll put her off the scent.

Her mother went off to make more food. Would she boil another egg, perhaps?

'Anything'll do, Mum. Jam . . . I'd love some jam on some toast.'

She had finished the sandwiches and drunk down the tea long before her mother had returned with a tray, half a loaf of bread, butter, strawberry jam, more tea.

'I don't like to think of you going without food,' she said.

'But I didn't, not really,' said Julie, remembering all the feasts she had had with Debbie, the pizzas that arrived all hours of the day and the night from almost next door, the Kentucky chicken, the special steak feeds when Debbie got hungry, which was often. In the little kitchen was a bowl from Morocco kept piled with fruit. 'You must get enough vitamins,' Debbie kept saying, and brought in more grapes, more apples and pears, let alone fruit Julie had never heard of, like pomegranates and pawpaws, which Debbie had learned to like on one of her trips somewhere.

'We aren't going to pester you with questions,' said her mother.

'I've been with a girl. Her name is Debbie. She was good to me. I've been all right,' said Julie, looking at her mother, and then at her father. *There, don't ask any more questions.*

'A girl?' said her father heavily. He still kept his eyes away from Julie, because when he looked at her the tears started up again.

'Well, I haven't been with a boyfriend,' said Julie and could not stop herself laughing at this ridiculous idea.

They were all laughing with relief, with disbelief . . . they think I've been off with a boy! What were they imagining? Julie contemplated the incident in the school cloakroom with Billy Jayson that so improbably had led

to the scene in the shed with the dog. She had joked with
Debbie that it would be a virgin birth. 'He hardly got
it in,' she had said. 'I didn't think anything had really
happened.'

Probably Billy had forgotten all about it. Unless he
connected her leaving school and running away from
home with that scene in the cloakroom? But why should
he? It was four months after they had tussled and shoved
and giggled, she saying, No no, and he saying, Oh come
on, then.

'Are you going back to school?' asked her mother carefully. 'The officer came round last week and said you still
could. There are two terms left. And you've always been
a good girl before this.'

'Yes, I'll go back,' said Julie. Seven months – she could
manage that. She'd be bored, but never mind. And then
. . . This was the moment she should say something more,
explain, make up some lies, for they both sat staring at her,
their faces full of what they had been feeling for the long
five months she had been gone. She knew she was treating
them badly, refusing to say anything. Well, she would, but
not now, she was suddenly absolutely exhausted. Full of
hot tea and food, she felt herself letting go, letting herself
slide . . . She began to yawn and could not stop. But they
did not suggest she should go to bed, and this was because
they simply could not believe they wouldn't get anything
more from her.

But there was nothing she could say. She looked at her
father, that cautious, greyish, elderly man, sitting heavily
in his chair. At her mother, who seemed almost girlish as
she sat upright there in her pretty pale blue dress with
its nice little collar and the little pearl buttons down the
front. Her grey curls were sprightly, and her blue eyes
full of wounded and uncomprehending innocence. Julie
thought, I wish I could just snuggle up to Mum and she

could hold me and I could go to sleep. Surely this must have happened when she was small, but she could not remember it. In this family, they simply did not touch each other.

Full of the clarity of her exhaustion, and because of what she had learned in the last months, she saw her parents and knew that – they cancelled each other out. Debbie would say there was something wrong with their chemistry. They did not disagree. They never raised their voices, or argued. Each day was a pattern of cups of tea, meals, cups of coffee and biscuits, always at exactly the same times, with bedtime as the goal. They seldom went out. They saw very few people, only each other. It was as if they had switched themselves off.

They had been old when she was born, was that the trouble?

At Debbie's people shouted, kissed, hugged, argued, fought, threatened, wept, and screamed.

There were two bedrooms in that flat. Debbie had given her the little one to herself. She was supposed to make herself scarce when Debbie came in with a man, a new one, but not when Derek was there, Debbie's real boyfriend. Derek joked a lot and ordered Julie about. How about making me a cup of tea, getting me a drink, making me some bacon and eggs, what have you been doing with yourself, why don't you get yourself a new hairdo, a new dress? He liked Julie, though she did not like him much. She knew he was not good enough for Debbie.

Soon Debbie would get rid of him. As she had the man who once owned the flat and took a percentage of what she earned. But Debbie had found out something bad about him, had put the screws on, got the flat for herself, worked for herself. Julie had seen this man just once, and he had given her the creeps. 'My first love,' Debbie joked, and laughed loudly when Julie grimaced.

Derek did not give her the creeps, he was just nothing!
Ordinary. Boring. But the man Debbie had gone to New
York with was a TV producer. He was making a series no
one had heard about in England, not good enough to sell
here, he said. This man was more like it, but Julie thought
Debbie would get rid of him too, when something better
came up.

All these thoughts, these judgments, so unlike anything
ever said or thought in her own home, went on in Julie's
mind quite comfortably, though they wouldn't do for
herself. Debbie had to be like this, because of her hard
life. This included something bad that Debbie had never
talked about, but it was why she had been so good to Julie.
Probably, just like Julie, Debbie had stood very late in a
railway station, pregnant, her head full of rubbish about
how she would get a job, have the baby, bring it up, find
a man who would love her and the baby. Or perhaps it
had been something else to do with being pregnant and
alone. It was not she, Julie, who had earned five months
of Debbie's love and protection, it was pregnant Julie,
helpless and alone.

Oh, yes, Debbie was fond of her.

Sometimes she spent the night in Debbie's big bed
because Debbie could not bear to sleep alone. She got
scared, she said. She could not believe that Julie wasn't
frightened of the dark. Debbie always crashed straight off
to sleep, even when she hadn't been drinking. Then Julie
cautiously got up on her elbow and bent over sleeping
Debbie, to examine her, try and find out . . . Debbie was
a big handsome girl. Her skin was very white, and she
had black shiny straight hair, and she made up her lips
to be thin and scarlet and curving, just right for the
lashing, slashing tongue behind them. When she was
asleep her face was smooth and closed, and her lips were
ordinary, quite pathetic Julie thought, and there was wear

under her eyes. That face showed nothing of why Debbie
said to people coming into the flat who might notice
Julie the wrong way, 'Lay off, do you hear? Lay off, or
I'll . . .' And her scarlet lips and her black eyes were nasty,
frightening.

But if Debbie woke in the night, she might turn to Julie
and draw her into an embrace that told Julie how little
she knew about love, about tenderness. Then Julie lay
awake, astounded at the revelations this big hot smooth
body made, and went on making, even though Debbie
was off to sleep again. She never actually 'did anything'.
Julie even waited for 'something' to happen. Nothing ever
did. Just once Debbie put her hand down to touch the
mound of Julie's stomach, but took it quickly away. Julie
lay entangled with Debbie, and they were like two cats
that have finished washing each other and gone to sleep,
and Julie knew how terribly she had been deprived at
home, and how empty and sad her parents were. Suppose
she said to her mother now, Mum, let me come into your
bed tonight, I'm scared, I've missed you . . . She could
just see her mother's embarrassed, timid face. 'But Julie,
you're a big girl now.'

Anne and Len slept in twin beds stretched out parallel
to each other, the night table between them.

There were tears in Julie's eyes, and she did not know
it, but then she did and looked quickly at her mother,
then her father, for they must not know she would give
anything to cry and cry, and be comforted and held . . .
But they weren't looking at her, only at the television. They
had switched it on, without her noticing. Now all three of
them sat staring at it.

On the screen a woman announcer smiled the special
smile that goes with royalty, animals, and children and
said, 'At eight o'clock this evening a newly born baby
girl was found in a telephone box in Islington. She was

warmly wrapped and healthy. She weighed seven pounds and three ounces. The nurses have called her Rosie.' Hot waves of jealousy went through Julie when she saw how the nurse smiled down at the little face seen briefly by Julie in torchlight, and then again through the sleet outside the shed. 'The mother is urged to come forward as she might be in need of urgent medical attention.'

It was the late news.

Surely they were going to guess? But why should they? It was hard enough for her to believe that she could sit here in her pretty little dressing gown smelling of bath powder, when she had given birth by herself in a dirty shed with only a dog for company. Four hours ago, that was all!

'Why don't we have a dog, Mum?' asked Julie, knowing what she was going to hear.

'But they are such a nuisance, Julie. And who's going to take it for walks?'

'I will, Mum.'

'But you'll have finished school in July, and I don't want the bother of a dog, and I'm sure Len doesn't.'

Her father didn't say anything. He leaned forward and turned off the set. The screen went blank.

'I often wonder what Jessie thinks,' he remarked, 'when she sees something like this on the telly, I mean.'

'Oh, leave it, Len,' said Anne warningly.

Julie did not really hear this, but then she did: her ears sprang to life, and she knew something extraordinary was about to happen.

'That's why we were so worried about you,' said Julie's father, heavy, grief-ridden, reproachful. 'It's easy enough to happen, how were we to know you weren't – '

'Len, we agreed we wouldn't ever – '

'What about Auntie Jessie?' asked Julie, trying to take it in. A silence. 'Well, what about her, Dad? You can't just leave it like that.'

'Len,' said Anne wildly.

'Your Auntie Jessie got herself into the family way,' said her father, determined to say it, ignoring his wife's face, her distress. His face was saying, Why should she be spared when she's given us such a bad time? 'She wasn't much older than you are now.' At last he was looking straight at Julie, full of reproach, and his eyes dripped tears all down his face and on to his tie. 'It can happen easy enough, can't it?'

'You mean . . . but what happened to the baby? Was it born?'

'Your cousin Freda,' said Len, still bitter and obstinate, his accusing eyes on his daughter.

'You mean, Freda is . . . you mean. Auntie Jessie's mum and dad didn't mind?'

'They minded, all right,' said Anne. 'I remember all that well enough. They wanted the baby adopted, but Jessie stuck it out and had it, and in the end they came around. I still think they were right and Jessie was wrong. She was only seventeen. She never would say who the father was. She was stuck at home with the baby when she should have been out enjoying herself and learning things. She got married when she was a baby herself.'

By now Julie was more or less herself again, though she felt as if she'd been on a roller coaster. Above all, what she was thinking was, I've got to get it all out of them now, because I know them, they'll clam up and never talk of it again.

'Didn't Uncle Bob mind?' she asked.

'Not so that he wouldn't marry her, he married her, didn't he, and she had a love child he had to take on,' said her father, full of anger and accusations.

'A love child,' said Julie derisively, unable to stop herself. But her parents didn't notice.

'That's what they call it, I believe,' said her father,

all heavy and sarcastic. 'Well, that's what can happen, Julie, and you've always been such a sensible girl and that made it worse.' And now, unbelievably, this father of hers, whom she had so feared she ran away from home, sat sobbing, covering his face with his hands.

Her mother was weeping, her eyes bright, her cheeks red.

In a moment Julie would be bawling too.

'I'm going to bed,' she said, getting up. 'Oh, I'm sorry Mum, I'm sorry, Dad, I'm sorry . . .'

'It's all right, Julie,' said her mother.

Julie went out of the room and up the stairs and into her room, walking carefully now, because she was so sore. And she felt numbed and confused, because of Aunt Jessica and her cousin Freda. Why, she, Julie, could have . . . she could be sitting here now, with her baby Rosie, they wouldn't have thrown her out.

She didn't know what to think, or to feel . . . She felt . . . she wanted . . . 'Oh, Debbie,' she cried, but silently, tucked into her little bed, her arms around the panda. 'Oh, Debbie, what am I to do?'

She thought, In July, when I've finished school, I am going back, I'm going to run away, I'll go to London and get a job, and I can have my baby. For a few minutes she persuaded herself it was not the silly little girl who had run away who said this, but the Debbie-taught girl who knew what things cost. Then she said to herself, Stop it, stop it, you know better.

She thought of Aunt Jessie's house. She had always enjoyed that house. It occurred to her now that Debbie's place and Aunt Jessie's had a lot in common – noisy, disturbing, exciting. Which was why her parents did not much like going there. But here, a baby here, Rosie with her long wrinkled cunt here . . . Julie was laughing her raucous, derisive laugh, but it was unhappy because she had understood that Rosie her daughter could not come here, because she, Julie, could not stand it.

I'll take Rosie to Debbie's in London, said Julie, in a final futile attempt.

But Debbie had taken in pregnant Julie. *That was what had been paid.*

If Julie brought baby Rosie here, then she would have to stay here. Until she got married. Like Auntie Jessie. Julie thought of Uncle Bob. Now she realized she had always seen him as Auntie Jessie's shadow, not up to much. She had wondered why Auntie Jessie married him. Now she knew.

I've got to get out of here, she thought, I've got to. In July I'll leave. I'll have my O levels. I can get them easily. I'll work hard and get my five O levels. I'll go to London. I know how things are, now. Look, I've lived in Debbie's flat, and I didn't let myself get hurt by them. I was clever, no one knew I was pregnant, only Debbie. I had Rosie by myself in that shed with only a dog to help me, and then I put Rosie in a safe place and now she's all right, and I've come home, and I've managed it all so well they never even guessed. I'm all right.

With her arms around the panda Julie thought, I can do anything I want to do, I've proved that.

And she drifted off to sleep.

Sparrows

Twenty minutes after the rain stopped, the first visitors came into the café garden. They were two elderly women and a smiling Labrador, very much at home, for they went straight to a certain table at the back, and the dog took his place on the grassy strip there without a command. The women tipped upright the chairs that had been slanted forward on to the table because of the rain. One hooked an umbrella on a chair-back and sat, bringing out packages of food from a holdall. The other went into the café building and emerged with one little coffeepot and two cups. Assuring each other that one pot was plenty for two, they ate sandwiches with a contemplative detached air that disdained guilt.

All over the northern reaches of London people were saying, 'The rain's stopped: let's go up to the Heath.' Already they wandered along the path where you can look down at the Kenwood lake, settled themselves on benches in case the sun did come out, and descended the stairs on the way to the café indoors. But where was the sun? It was sulking behind banks of black cloud, sliding for minutes at a time to their edges from where it stained trees and grass a promising sultry yellow, but then withdrew.

Some teenagers emerged from the building balancing trays loaded with fizzy drinks, coffee, cake. They pushed two tables together and sat sprawling. Elegant, dramatic clothes, profuse and many coloured hair, created a festive occasion. Their discontented indolence – their style – caused the two frugal observers to raise eyebrows and murmur, 'Some people don't know when they're lucky, do they, dear?'

A tall, pale, straw-haired youth like a ballet dancer appeared at the kitchen door. He was all yawns and sleep, but he was adjusting a blue and white striped apron, and this transformed him into the picture of a willing waiter. He surveyed his scene of operations, pondering whether to straighten the chairs around tables that had pools of rainwater on them, or even to wipe the tables. But he cocked an eye at the ominous sky and decided not to bother.

The two ladies were throwing bits of sandwich to sparrows that gathered around their feet, crowded the backs of chairs and even ventured on their table. At the end of the garden, not too emphatically displayed, a board said, PUBLIC HEALTH NOTICE. IN THE INTERESTS OF HYGIENE PLEASE DO NOT FEED THE BIRDS. The waiter shrugged and disappeared.

Three people appeared from inside, almost obscured by the heaped trays they bore, but when these were set down, three Japanese were revealed, a young couple in smart black silk jumpsuits, and the mother of one of them. She too was overdressed for this place in black 'designer' clothes, jewellery, the lot. They pulled a table near the one they had chosen to sit at in the middle of the scene, to hold all that they carried and what was on the tray brought to them by another waiter. This buffet not being enough, a second table was brought close and covered with food. They were about to eat full English breakfasts, wedges of cream cake, scones and butter and jam, several other kinds of cake, plates of salad and chicken, and, as well, coffee, Coca-Cola, fruit juice.

The waiter who was from somewhere around the Mediterranean, a dark, lithe, handsome youth, surveyed this repast with admiring incredulity. 'Japanese? Good appetite!' He lingered, raised his brows in private exclamation, and went off. The sparrows, having exhausted the amenities of the two pensioners, arrived in a flock to examine new possibilities. The Japanese mother let out cries of angry indignation, stuffing her highly made-up face ugly with bad temper and greed, with one hand, while she swatted ineffectively with the other at the sparrows as if they were flies.

The teenagers clearly felt they were being forced to examine all this from much too close so they gracefully rose and removed themselves to several tables away. They did not bother to take all their food and left crisps and peanuts all over their deserted table. The sparrows fell on this bounty, arriving from trees, roof – everywhere. The Japanese matron loudly commented on this, but her children ignored her, eating as if they had been deprived of food for weeks.

The two elderly ladies watched this scene. They did not seem able to take their eyes off it. Their disapproval of the teenagers had been ritual, even indulgent, but this – their expressions said – was something else! One of them put down a hand that trembled, and stroked the big dog's head.

'There you are, good dog,' she said in an unhappy voice. A sparrow arrived too close to the Japanese matron and she let out a shout. Still another waiter arrived at the kitchen door and examined the scene like a general. A short, stocky, competent youth, his hair brushed straight up, everything about him neat and clean, he was obviously destined to be running his own firm or at least a department within, at the most, five years. He strode forcefully about, scattering clouds of sparrows by flinging out his arms energetically as if he were doing exercises. He smiled with a nod at the Japanese and went back into the kitchen. The sparrows returned.

A middle-aged couple shining with health and sun-tan lotion arrived, each holding one austere cup of coffee. They had evidently just come back from a holiday in the blissful sun, and could afford to smile now at where it hid behind a bank of black that covered half the sky. They put their cups on either side of a small lake of rainwater on their table, and sat on the edge of their chairs in a way that told everybody they were about to demolish the distances of the Heath at a dedicated trot.

The middle-aged couple that arrived now couldn't be more unlike them. They walked cautiously up the steps and came forward, watching how they set down their well-cleaned shoes. Each carried a tray with tea and a single scone and butter. They chose a table at the back, near the little grassy strip.

Behind them was the tall brick wall with its mysterious, always-closed door, like the Secret Garden. The woman sat stirring her tea, while she smiled at the Labrador, then at the banks of bushes and trees on the right, all shades of heavy, lush green, then at the tops of the trees that showed over the palisade on the left, finally looking straight ahead with approval at the long shapely building, a wing of Kenwood House, once a coach house and servants' quarters, that was now rapidly filling with people having breakfast, tea and lunch. The open upper windows hinted at the satisfactorily interesting lives going on inside, and on the long, low, roof, birds of all kinds, but mostly sparrows and pigeons, carried on their no less interesting affairs. She regarded with particular appreciation the sparrows who crowded a tree just behind them, watching for what might befall them next. Her husband was already leaning forward to consume his scone in the fussy, urgent way of a man who would always attend to whatever was in front of him, finish it, and then wonder why he had been in such a hurry.

A sparrow dropped from the tree and sat on the back of the tilted-forward chair next to the woman. She carefully pushed some crumbs towards it.

'Hilda, what are you doing!' expostulated her husband in a low, urgent, peevish voice. 'It's not allowed, is it?' And he craned his neck around to assure himself the Public Health Notice was still safely there.

'Oh well, but that's just silly,' said she serenely, smiling at the sparrow. He glared at her, a piece of scone halfway to his mouth, with the frustrated look of one who did not feel in control of anything. Then, as the sparrow fluttered cheekily towards his hand and the scone, he stuffed it in, swallowed it, and said, 'They'd steal the food out of your mouth.'

Hilda gently set the tilted chair upright, and then the one next to it. At once sparrows descended to sit on their backs. She put a crumb quite close to her and sat waiting. A seasoned sparrow, one of many summers, a lean hunting bird, grey blotched with chocolate and black, darted in, snatched it, and flew off to the roof of the coach house, with two others in pursuit.

On the back of the chair nearest to her three sparrows sat watching, side by side.

'Look, Alfred,' she said, 'they are babies: look, they've still got a bit of their gape left.'

The corners of their beaks were yellow. All three were

neat and fresh. New-minted. Their greyish-brown feathers glistened. The man was staring at them with a look of
apprehension too strong for the occasion.

From a distance this man seemed younger than he was, a
sprightly middle age, being cleaned and brushed and tidy,
but from close you could see fresh crumbs on his cardigan,
and a new tea stain on his tie. He had a greyish, drained
look. His wife was a large full-fleshed woman who sat up
straight there beside him, everything about her showing
she was in command, her hands kept and capable, hair
neatly waved, clothes just so. If she was not much younger
than he was, then that was what she seemed.

She laid some crumbs close to the three birds and the
boldest hesitated, darted in, and flew off with one. The
second fought with himself, took off from the chair-back,
but halfway to the crumb, his goal, panic overtook him,
and with a swirl and a flutter of wings he turned in mid-air
and returned to the chair-back.

'Go on, be a brave bird,' she admonished it. Again the
hesitant take-off, the mid-air swerve and whirl of wings
when for a few seconds it hovered, then retreated. At last
this sparrow managed to overcome its fear and resist the
need to turn back halfway, and he reached the crumb
and showed he would have a successful future because
he picked up several, very fast, and flew off somewhere
with a full beak to enjoy them.

The remaining sparrow sat on there, alone. He was very
new, this little one, with remnants of baby fluff showing
here and there. The yellow corners of his beak were bright.
He had been sitting watching his fellow ex-fledglings
with the calm, round-eyed, detached look of a baby in
a pram.

'Come on, you do it too,' she said. But the little bird sat
on there, watching, not involved at all.

Then a new bird arrived on the table among the crumbs,

and pecked as fast as it could. It was an older bird, its feathers no longer fresh and young. And now the little sparrow hopped on to the table, crouched, fluffed out its feathers so that it became a soft ball, and opened its beak.

'What's the matter with it?' demanded the man, as if in a panic. 'It's sick.'

'No, no,' soothed his wife. 'Watch.'

The older bird at once responded to the smaller bird's crouching and fluffing by stuffing crumbs into its gape. This went on, the baby demanding, as if still in its nest, and the parent pushing in crumbs. But then a brigand sparrow came swooping in. The parent sparrow pecked it and the two quarrelling birds flew off together to the roof. The little sparrow, abandoned, stopped cowering and spreading its feathers. It closed its beak, returned to the chair-back and resumed its bland baby pose.

'But it's grown-up,' said the man, full of resentment. 'It's grown-up and it expects its parents to feed it.'

'It was probably still a baby in its nest yesterday,' she said. 'This is probably its first day out in the wicked world.'

'Why isn't it feeding itself, then? If the parents have pushed it out, then it should be supporting itself.'

She turned her head to give him a wary glance, removed this diagnostic inspection as if she feared his reaction to it, and sat with a bit of scone in her hand, watching the throng of sparrows who were looting the now empty plates and platters of the Japanese trio. The Japanese matron was grumbling loudly about the birds. Her children pacified her, and waved to the indolent waiter with the shock of straw hair, who came across at his leisure, piled up trays, and went off with them, depriving the sparrows of their buffet. They whirled up into the air and the baby sparrow went with them.

The little garden café was filling with people. The sun was again close to the edge of the clouds, and one half of the sky was bright blue. The athletic couple went striding efficiently away. The young male Japanese went back into the building. Surely he wasn't prepared to tackle even more food? The two elderly ladies sat on, though a waiter had removed their coffeepot and the two empty plates.

The dog lay with its chin on the grass and watched a sparrow hopping about within inches of him.

The baby sparrow returned by itself to sit on the chair-back.

'Look, it's back,' she said, full of tenderness. 'It's the baby.'

'How do you know it's the same one?'

'Can't you see it is?'

'They all look alike to me.'

She said nothing, but began her game of carefully pushing crumbs nearer and nearer to it, so that it would be tempted but not frightened.

'I suppose it's waiting for its father to come and feed it,' came the grumble which her alert but cautious pose said she had expected.

'Or perhaps even its mother,' she said, dry, ironic – but regretted this note as soon as the words were out, for he erupted loudly, 'Sitting there, just waiting for us to . . .'

She said carefully, 'Look, Father, I said this morning, if you don't want to do it, then you don't have to.'

'You'd never let me forget it then, would you!'

She said nothing, but leaned gently to push a crumb closer to the bird.

'And then if I didn't I suppose she'd be back home, expecting us to wait on her, buying her food . . .'

She was counting ten before she spoke. 'That's why she wants to leave and get a place of her own.'

'At our expense.'

'The money's only sitting in the bank.'

'But suppose we wanted it for something. Repairs to the house . . . the car's getting old . . .'

She sighed, not meaning to. 'I said, if you feel like that about it, then don't. But it's only £10,000. That's not much to put down to begin on getting independent. It's a very good deal, you said that yourself. She'll own a bit of something, even if it is only a share of the place.'

'I don't see we've any choice. Either we have her at home feeding her and all her friends and Uncle Tom Cobbleigh and all, or we have to pay to get her out.'

'She's twenty-one,' said the mother, suddenly exhausted with anger, her voice low and tight. 'It's time we did something for her.'

He heard, and was going to retreat, but said first, 'It's the legal age, isn't it? She's an adult, not a baby.'

She did not reply.

Out came the Japanese young man with yet another tray. More cakes piled with cream and jam, more coffee. As soon as he had set these down before his wife (girlfriend? sister?) and his (her?) mother, the three of them bent over and began eating as if in an eating contest.

'They aren't short of what it needs,' he grumbled.

That peevish old voice: it was the edge of senility. Soon she would be his nurse. She was probably thinking something like this while she smiled, smiled, at the bird.

'Come on,' she whispered, 'it's not difficult.'

And then . . . the baby hopped down on to the table with its round eyes fixed on her, clumsily took up a crumb, swallowed it.

'Very likely that's the first time it has ever done that for itself,' she whispered, and her eyes were full of tears. 'The little thing . . .'

The small sparrow was pecking in an experimental way. Then it got the hang of it, and soon became as voracious as its elders as she pushed crumbs towards it. Then it had cleaned up the table top and was off – an adult.

'Marvellous,' she said. 'Wonderful. Probably even this morning it was still in its nest and now . . .' And she laughed, with tears in her eyes.

He was looking at her. For the first time since they had sat down there he was outside his selfish prison and really seeing her.

But he was seeing her not as she was now, but at some time in the past. A memory . . .

'It's a nice little bird,' he said, and when she heard that voice from the past, not a semi-senile whine, she turned and smiled full at him.

'Oh it's so wonderful,' she said, vibrating with pleasure. 'I love this place. I love . . .' And indeed the sun had come out, filling the green garden with summer, making people's faces shine and smile.

*T*he Mother
o f the Child
in Question

High on a walkway connecting two tower blocks Stephen
Bentley, social worker, stopped to survey the view. Cement,
everywhere he looked. Stained grey piles went up into
the sky, and down below lay grey acres where only one
person moved among puddles, soft drink cans and bits
of damp paper. This was an old man with a stick and a
shopping bag. In front of Stephen, horizontally dividing
the heavy building from pavement to low cloud, were
rows of many-coloured curtains where people kept out of
sight. They were probably watching him, but he had his
credentials, the file under his arm. The end of this walkway
was on the fourth floor. The lift smelled bad: someone had
been sick in it. He walked up grey urine-smelling stairs to
the eighth floor, Number 15. The very moment he rang, the
door was opened by a smiling brown boy. This must be
Hassan, the twelve-year-old. His white teeth, his bright
blue jersey, the white collar of his shirt, all dazzled, and
behind him the small room crammed with furniture was
too tidy for a family room, everything just so, polished,
shining. Thorough preparations had been made for this
visit. In front of a red plush sofa was the oblong of a low
table, and on it waited cups, saucers and a sugar bowl full

to the brim. A glinting spoon stood upright in it. Hassan sat down on the sofa, smiling hard. Apart from the sofa, there were three chairs, full of shiny cushions. In one of them sat Mrs Khan, a plump pretty lady wearing the outfit Stephen thought of as 'pyjamas' – trousers and tunic in flowered pink silk. They looked like best clothes, and the ten-year-old girl in the other chair wore a blue tunic and trousers, with earrings, bangles and rings. Mother wore a pink gauzy scarf, the child a blue one. These, in Pakistan, would be there ready to be pulled modestly up at the sight of a man, but here they added to the festive atmosphere. Stephen sat down in the empty chair at Mrs Khan's (Stephen particularly noted) peremptory gesture. But she smiled. Hassan smiled and smiled. The little girl had not, it seemed, noticed the visitor, but she smiled too. She was pretty, like a kitten.

'Where is Mr Khan?' asked Stephen of Mrs Khan, who nodded commandingly at her son. Hassan at once said, 'No, he cannot come, he is at work.'

'But he told me he would be here. I spoke to him on the telephone yesterday.'

Again the mother gave Hassan an order with her eyes, and he said, smiling with all his white teeth, 'No, he is not here.'

In the file that had the name Shireen Khan on the front, the last note, dated nine months before, said, 'Father did not keep appointment. His presence essential.'

Mrs Khan said something in a low voice to her son, who allowed the smile to have a rest just as long as it took to fetch a tray with a pot of tea on it, and biscuits, from the sideboard. They must have been watching from the windows and made the tea when they saw him down there, file under his arm. Hassan put the smile back on his face when he sat down again. Mrs Khan poured strong tea. The boy handed Stephen a cup, and the plate of biscuits.

Mrs Khan set a cup before her daughter, and counted five
biscuits on to a separate plate and put this near the cup.
The little girl was smiling at – it seemed – attractive private
fancies. Mrs Khan clicked her tongue with annoyance and
said something to her in Urdu. But Shireen took no notice.
She was bursting with internal merriment, and the result
of her mother's prompting was that she tried to share this
with her brother, reaching out to poke him mischievously,
and laughing. Hassan could not prevent a real smile at her,
tender, warm, charmed. He instantly removed this smile
and put back the polite false one.

'Five,' said Mrs Khan in English. 'She can count. Say
five, Shireen.' It was poor English, and she repeated the
command in Urdu.

The little girl smiled delightfully and began breaking
up the biscuits and eating them.

'If your husband would agree to it, Shireen could go to
the school we discussed – my colleague William Smith
discussed with you – when he came last year. It is a
good school. It would cost a little but not much. It is
Government-funded but there is a small charge this year.
Unfortunately.'

Mrs Khan said something sharp and the boy translated.
His English was fluent. 'It is not money. My father has
the money.'

'Then I am sorry but I don't understand. The school
would be good for Shireen.'

Well, within limits. In the file was a medical report,
part of which read, 'The child in question would possibly
benefit to a limited extent from special tuition.'

Mrs Khan said something loud and angry. Her amiable face was twisted with anger. Anxiety and anger had
become the air in this small overfilled overclean room, and
now the little girl's face was woeful and her lips quivered.
Hassan at once put out his hand to her and made soothing

noises. Mrs Khan tried simultaneously to smile at the child
and show a formal cold face to the intrusive visitor.

Hassan said, 'My mother says Shireen must go to the
big school, Beavertree School.'

'Is that where you go, Hassan?'

'Yes, sir.'

'My name is Stephen, Stephen Bentley.'

'Yes, sir.'

'Your father should be here,' said Stephen, trying not
to sound peevish. There was something going on, but he
could not make out what. If it wasn't that two daughters
were doing well at school Stephen would have thought
perhaps Mr Khan was old-fashioned and didn't want
Shireen educated. (The two girls were both older than
Hassan, but being girls did not count. It was the oldest
son who had to be here representing the father.) Not that
there was any question of 'educating' Shireen. So what
was it? Certainly he had sounded perfunctory yesterday
on the telephone, agreeing to be here today.

Mrs Khan now took out a child's picture book she had
put down the side of the armchair for this very moment,
and held it in front of Shireen. It was a brightly coloured
book, for a three-year-old, perhaps. Shireen smiled at it
in a vacant willing way. Mrs Khan turned the big pages,
frowning and nodding encouragingly at Shireen. Then
she made herself smile. The boy was smiling away like
anything. Shireen was happy and smiling.

'Look,' said Stephen, smiling but desperate, 'I'm not
saying that Shireen will learn to read well, or anything
like that, but . . .'

At this Mrs Khan slammed the book shut and faced him.
No smiles. A proud, cold, stubborn woman, eyes flashing,
she demolished him in Urdu.

Hassan translated the long tirade thus. 'My mother says
Shireen must go to the big school with the rest of us.'

'But, Mrs Khan, she can't go to the big school. How can she?' As Mrs Khan did not seem to have taken this in, he addressed the question again to Hassan. 'How can she go to the big school? It's not possible!'

Hassan's smile was wan, and Stephen could swear there were tears in his eyes. But he turned his face away.

Another angry flood from Mrs Khan, but Hassan did not interpret. He sat silent and looked sombrely at the chuckling and delighted little girl who was stirring biscuit crumbs around her plate with her finger. Mrs Khan got up, full of imperious anger, pulled Shireen up from her chair, and went stormily out of the room, tugging the child after her by the hand. Stephen could hear her exclaiming and sighing and moving around the next room, and addressing alternately admonishing and tender remarks to the child. Then she wept loudly.

Hassan said, 'Excuse me, sir, but I must go to my school. I asked permission to be here, and my teacher said yes, but I must go back quickly.'

'Did your father tell you to be here?'

Hassan hesitated. 'No, sir. My mother said I must be here.'

For the first time Hassan was really looking at him. It even seemed that he might say something, explain . . . His eyes were full of a plea. For understanding? There was pride there, hurt.

'Thank you for staying to interpret, Hassan,' said the social worker. 'I wish I could talk to your father . . .'

'Excuse me, excuse me,' said Hassan, and went running out. Stephen called, 'Goodbye, Mrs Khan,' got no reply, and followed the boy. Along the dismal, stained and smelly corridors. Down the grey cement stairs. On to the walkway. A wind was blowing, fresh and strong. He looked down and saw Hassan four storeys below, a small urgent figure racing across the cement, leaping

puddles, kicking bits of paper. He reached the street and
vanished. He was running from a situation he hated: his
whole body shouted it. What on earth . . . Just *what* was
all that about?

And then Stephen understood. Suddenly. Just like that.
But he couldn't believe it. But yes, he had to believe it. No,
it wasn't possible . . .

Not impossible. It was true.

Mrs Khan did not know that Shireen was 'subnormal'
as the medical record put it. She was not going to admit
it. Although she had two normal sons and two normal
daughters, all doing well at school, and she knew what
normal bright children were like, she was not going
to make the comparison. For her, Shireen was normal.
No good saying this was impossible. For Stephen was
muttering, 'No, it simply isn't *on*, it's crazy.' Anyway,
he found these 'impossibilities' in his work every day. A
rich and various lunacy inspired the human race and you
could almost say the greater part of his work was dealing
with this lunacy.

Stephen stood clutching the balustrade and gripping the
file, because the wind was swirling noisily around the high
walkway. His eyes were shut because he was examining in
his mind's eye the picture of Mrs Khan's face, that proud,
cold, refusing look. So would a woman look while her
husband shouted at her, 'You stupid woman, she can't
go to the big school with the others, why are you so
stubborn? Do I have to explain it to you again?' She
must have confronted her husband with this look and her
silence a hundred times! And so he had not turned up for
the appointment, or for the other appointment, because he
knew it was no good. He didn't want to have to say to some
social worker, 'My wife's a fine woman, but she has this
little peculiarity!' And Hassan wasn't going to say, 'You
see, sir, there's a little problem with my mother.'

Stephen, eyes still shut, went on replaying what he had seen in that room: the tenderness on Mrs Khan's face for her afflicted child, the smile on the boy's face, the real, warm, affectionate smile, at his sister. The little girl was swaddled in their tenderness, the family adored her, what was she going to learn at the special school better than she was getting from her family?

Stephen found he was filling with emotions that threatened to lift him off the walkway with the wind and float him off into the sky like a balloon. He wanted to laugh, or clap his hands, or sing with exhilaration. That woman, that *mother*, would not admit her little girl was simple. She just wouldn't agree to it! Why, it was a wonderful thing, a miracle! Good for you, Mrs Khan, said Stephen Bentley opening his eyes, looking at the curtained windows four floors above him where he had no doubt Mrs Khan was watching him, proud she had won yet another victory against those busybodies who would class her Shireen as stupid.

'Bloody marvellous,' shouted the social worker into the wind. He opened his file against his knee then and there and wrote, 'Father did not turn up as arranged. His presence essential.' The date. His own name.

Pleasures of the Park

An elderly man stood with his face to the wire of the bird enclosure. Everything about him was yellowish and dry, like a fungus on an old log, but even his back was full of the vitality of indignation. In the enclosure live flamingos and demoiselle cranes, but he was looking at a fowl, a chicken, a rooster like a sunset in the act of exploding, all iridescent black, gold and scarlet, a resplendent cock who sat on a shiny log raising its wings and crowing, a triumphal shout. 'You shut up,' threatened the man through the wire. The cock riposted, 'Cock-a-doodle-doo,' or, perhaps, 'Cock-a-rico,' and the man said, 'What are you so pleased with yourself about?' – at which, 'Crack-acrack-ooow,' said the cock, lifting himself a few inches into the air and settling again. 'Cock-a-rooi!' 'Just you shut up,' said the man. People were looking humorous and pointing him out. He realized this, and turned, squaring his shoulders and glaring. Then off he marched, one-two, one-two, through the trees. The cock shook scarlet wattles and stepped daintily off his log.

Not far away is the paddock where the deer and the goats are kept. At that wire generations of children have learned their parents' attitudes to the animals. 'Nasty

vicious things, goats,' says mummy, out of centuries-old
memories of goat as Lucifer, goat as witches' friend, goat
driven away under its load of sins, and a little boy says,
'Nasty goats.' Or, 'Darling, look at that lovely little kid.'
But everybody loves the deer.

Deer and goats coexist. The goats are dominant. If
goodies are being offered, carrots, apples, bread, then
even the big stags will allow themselves to be shouldered
aside by goats a third their size. If the goats are replete
the stags command the fences. Then come the females, in
order of their size and weight and, perhaps, even of their
personalities. Behind the deer stand last year's fawns,
while this year's, who still have their bambi foreheads
(Ohhhh, look at the bambis!), stand about at the back
watching their elders crowd forward to get titbits. But
what the babies like best is to jump into the air on some
impulse and then prance madly across the field.

The deer herd disposes itself according to rules we may
only guess at. Sometimes the two stags lie among their
subjects, regal creatures, holding about them atmospheres
from when kings and courts hunted them, and from
before that, when shamans were deer, became them in
ceremonies going back thousands of years, horns bound to
their foreheads. And when did foreheads sprouting horns
become ribald?

Sometimes the two stags repose by themselves, or
browse side by side, seeming disdainful or indifferent,
while the does and fawns lie about or feed together.
Sometimes, when the fawns are new, mothers and babies
make a nursery place under the enormous oak, while the
females too young to breed and the last season's babies
are near, but separate. Last year seven fawns were born,
and the year before, seven. These surges of population
cannot be accommodated, and one may arrive at the fence
among all the little boys and girls who have been given

carrot sticks or who have tugged up bits of grass, to find
that in the night Fate has struck in the shape of a van, and
borne off half a dozen or more of the herd. Where have they
gone? Anguishing thoughts, better not pursued. Special
friends – vanished. The white doe whose this year's fawn
learned trust for humans from her has gone, though the
fawn is still here. And the infant stag, whose buds were
just showing? And five of last year's children? But the
opposite also happens. The autumn before last, overnight,
instead of seven fawns suddenly there were twelve, for
clearly this benign place is regarded by Them, by the
Fates, as a satisfactory nursery. Somewhere, in another
paddock or forest or zoo, bereft does are looking for their
fawns, who are prancing about here.

There are always two stags. Why two? Some lore of deer
breeding must order two males for a herd. They are not
friends at rutting time. As I write the second stag is sad,
is desolate, stands with his head lowered, all by himself,
refuses our offerings, and people can be heard, 'Oh, poor
Rudolph, are you sick?' No, he is not sick. The Master
Buck is standing on a little eminence, turning his great
antlers about, tossing them, raking the grass with them,
emitting grunting roars, and a reek of musk. Second Buck
is being hustled away every time he approaches a female,
he is being taught every minute of this long October that
he is inferior. Sometimes animals emanate depression as
humans do.

Soon, those now eroded and splintering antlers will fall
off. The two stags will be hornless among their females, to
be distinguished from them by their neck and shoulder
muscles. And then . . . then . . . oh, miracles, the new
horns appear, pulsing and velvety buds, and soon become
like bars or handles, soft as moss to the touch, and branch,
and rush up out of those tender heads and in no time there
they are, the new antlers.

Astonishing events may be observed, to be interpreted anthropomorphically or not, according to taste. The summer before last, in July, it happened that we arrived at the fence as a female was giving birth. The bloody bundle dropped from the rear end of a pretty young doe, and she was turning to smell it just as her last year's fawn, now a half-sized beast, came running. It was demented with jealousy. It knocked over the baby struggling to its feet, and began pursuing the mother around the great paddock. The poor beast, exhausted by the birth, the afterbirth protruding, was harried and hurried all around the field, sometimes staggering and letting out cries of distress. The fawn who had lost its place with her because of this birth would not let her rest nor come near the new fawn. The afterbirth tumbled. At once the crows swooped in to clean up. Meanwhile the two stags who had apparently taken no notice of all this where they lay under the oak got to their feet. First Master Buck, then Second Buck, followed by half a dozen females, walked at their leisure to the fawn lying abandoned in the grass. The two big males stood over the baby. They turned their heads to observe the mother who was still being harried by the jealous pricket. Then Master Buck bent his great head and nosed the baby to its feet. It staggered. It fell. Master Buck again put his nose under the fawn and held it up. It stood, and for longer this time. Then it collapsed. But the males and the females were satisfied. They strolled off to the fence and stood accepting bits of this and that from human friends. When we left half an hour later the mother was still trying to evade her last year's fawn, hoarsely protesting, and sometimes falling.

Next day she was suckling the baby, but the displaced year-old, the pricket, was close, and she kept moving to keep herself between him, or her, and the fawn.

The goats, too, are not without their dramas. This year two of them were mated, solid matrons, put into a small subsidiary paddock that has its own shed, with a billy goat. This surprised us, for the nannies are so fat, with all the bread and vegetables, that they seem permanently pregnant, but only two were supplied with a mate. When they rejoined the flock in the big field they quickly expanded like inflatables. Until – look! – she's had a baby. One of them had given birth to a little black and white creature, cocky and cheeky from the first breath. It jumped up the exposed roots of the big oak and stood there showing off, I am king of the castle. Then it ran down and presented a lowered forehead to a big goat, many times its size, who accepted the challenge and carefully put its own forehead down and allowed the baby to butt. The alarmed mother watched the contest but soon could not stand it, and interposed herself between the large goat and the kid who, all sauce and derring-do, kept swaggering up to this big goat and then another, put down its curly forehead and played at butting, anxious mamma always in attendance.

And the second nanny goat? Something must have happened. For a long time she was shut in the enclosure, her swollen udder like bagpipes, looking out at the other mother and the baby. At last her udder subsided. (Was she being milked? Was Nature doing all it ought?) Soon, childless, she was back with the others.

The crows are around all the time, sitting about in the big trees, or on the ground, where they flop and waddle about, searching for what might be in the droppings, or for overlooked bits of bread. The crows would have the eyes out of the fawns' heads if the mothers were not vigilant. But while mamma goats and the does keep a sharp eye out for crows sidling too close to their offspring, you may very well see on a deer stretched out resting in the grass a crow picking off flies and other insects that plague deer and goats through the long hot months. And we have had two good summers, bringing the insects out in swarms.

Thus, in Africa, one may see tick birds picking insects off
the hides of animals.

In a week or so the leaves will be down off the trees
around the animals' enclosure, and the crows and the
other birds will be visible, many of them, too many, for
the mild winters have exploded the bird populations. I
counted a hundred crows last week as I threw them bits
of bread and they were still flying in from every part of the
sky. It seems there is a crow appointed – or self-appointed
– to summon the others, for there is a characteristic cry that
sounds like 'Quick, here's food'. Interesting that during
the last severe winter when the birds had such a bad time
I put down in my packed-with-ice garden bits of offal for
the crows, but they preferred bread. First they ate up the
bread, consuming half a dozen loaves in five minutes and
then they ate up the meat. *O.E.D. Raptores: The name of
an order of birds of prey, including the eagle, hawk, buzzard,
owl etc.* Who, one may assume, would take to sliced white
bread if offered it?

So there are the wild animals behind their fence. On the
free side humans – and dogs. The deer don't like it when
dogs come nosing up to their fence. Sometimes they see
dogs where no dogs are. I have a brown woolly coat which
I may bundle under my arm, and then the deer and the
crows keep their distance. Clearly they are seeing a brown
furry animal. If I wear the coat, filling it out with a human
shape, it is all right.

The dogs are teased by the wire. They nose about,
trying to remember what their relationships really are
with the creatures whose smells start ancestral reminiscences. 'Come away,' shout their owners. 'Come here,
Bonzo! Millie! Trixie!' Every weekend the parks fill with
dogs, and this park, an outflank of the Heath, one of the
pleasantest, is populated with dogs who have probably
spent a sad week shut in houses or even flats, let out,

but let out conditionally, off the leash for such a short time and then on sufferance. Dogs who have hardly seen another dog since they were removed from their mother's teats and their siblings' play see everywhere big dogs and little dogs, dogs like themselves. 'Hey, wait a minute – ' their instincts whisper to them, 'a dog does not necessarily have to be a human appendage.' The dogs approach each other, wagging their tails: they sniff bottoms, standing still to be sniffed, or going around in circles while the others nose after infatuating smells – smells that explode in their brains with instructions that contradict everything they have been taught. A dog approaches another with a stick, or with an inviting bark: Come and play, come and chase me. At once a dozen dogs of all sizes are running about and chasing each other, their barks sounding like shouts of joy. These dogs may be descendants of the descendants of house-bound, human-bound dogs, but already they are a pack: you can see the boss dog, and the pack order forming . . . you can see how they would be left to themselves to forage and chase and fight. And you feel in yourself instincts as old as theirs, when a wolf howling on a hungry winter's night lifted the hair on your ancestors' necks. But . . . here come the owners, here are the humans, they come running to establish order. 'Come here at once, Bonzo! Gruff! Fifi! Lulu! . . . Bad dog! To heel!' The pack falls apart and the dogs return soberly to their owners. 'Good dog. Good dog!' And they fall in behind human legs, sniffing at human hands which pat and caress and set down plates of food. But as they go they turn their heads to look back at the other, forbidden dogs. And this look is not only wistful but puzzled.

There is a bear-sized black dog that comes to the café on the hill where I and friends have spent so many happy hours. As it approaches, heads may turn, there may be frissons of alarm from those who have not before seen the beast. The monster dog sits obediently by a chair while its family goes off to get coffee and cakes. The dog, its lolling tongue like a pink plastic tie, seems to smile as it waits. Here they are, his family! They have brought him an ice-cream. He opens jaws like a bear's ... the ice-cream slides from the cone to the great pink tongue, he delicately swallows, and the cone follows. He flops his black furry tail about and lies down. During the very hot days of last summer two enormous black dogs walked into the pond near the bridge, and they sat like bears in arm chairs, lapping at the ripples, smiling while their young mistress called, 'Come on, Bruno, come on out of there, Baxter!' But they took no notice, sitting on their backsides in cool mud, their paws flopping in the water under their chins, looking guilty but not enough to bring them out of the deliciousness into the day's heat. 'Come on *out*, Bruno, Baxter!' They stayed put, cheerfully naughty dogs.

Womb Ward

Eight beds in a large room, four on either side and too close to each other. This was a shabby Victorian hospital in North London, and probably the room had not been designed as a ward. But it was decent, with pink flowery curtains at the windows, and on runners to separate the beds for moments needing privacy. Because the room was tidied for visiting time the long decorous swathes of pink were tied back. A lot of people sat about on chairs or on the beds. Mothers and sisters, brothers and cousins, friends and children had been coming and going since two in the afternoon. Not the husbands: they would be in later. But there was one husband who sat close to the head of a bed where a pretty woman of about forty-five lay turned towards him. She gazed into his face while he held both her hands, one in each of his. They were large hands, and he was a big man, wearing good clothes, tweedy grey jacket and a white shirt that dazzled, like those in the advertisements. But he had taken off his tie, which hung on his chair back, and this gave him an informal look. The intensity of his concern for his wife and her imploring gaze at him isolated them as if a curtain had gone up on them in their own home.

Certainly neither was aware of the visitors who came
and went.

He had brought her in at midday and had been sitting
with her ever since, before formal visiting hours began.

This was a ward for gynaecological problems, or, as the
women joked, a womb ward. The seven other women had
had or would have operations or other treatment. No one
was seriously ill, and more joking went on than in any
other kind of ward, yet low spirits were never far away,
and the nurses who were always in and out kept an eye
open for a woman weeping, or one silent for too long.

At six o'clock the suppers were brought in and most
visitors went home. No one had an appetite, but the
husband coaxed his wife to eat while she protested she
did not want to. She cried a little but stopped when he
soothed her like a father, and she sat obediently with a
bowl of custard in her hand while he fed her with a spoon
from it, sometimes putting down the spoon to blot her
eyes with a large old-fashioned very white handkerchief,
for she could not keep back the tears for long. She wept
like a child with little gulps and snuffles and heaves of her
chest, always watching him with her wide wet blue eyes.
Blue eyes meant to be happy, for crying did not suit her.

The other women watched this scene. Sometimes their
gazes met, commenting on it. Then husbands came in after
work, and for an hour or so the room contained couples in
close practical talk about children and domestic matters.
Four husbands had come. One old woman sat alone,
turning the pages of a magazine and watching the others
over it. Another, Miss Cook, had never been married. She,
too, watched what went on, while she knitted. The third
who had no man beside her read a book and listened to
her Walkman. She was 'the horsey one'. (Whether she was
horsey or not no one knew: she was presumed to be, being
upper-class.)

Then it was time for the men to leave, and they went: kisses, waves, see you tomorrow. The woman who had come that day clung to her husband and wept. 'Oh don't go, don't go, Tom, please don't go.' He held her and stroked her back, her shoulders, her soft grey nicely waved hair, now in disorder. He repeated, 'I must go, dear. Please stop crying, Mildred, you must pull yourself together, please, dear.' But she saw no reason to stop. She lifted her face to show a mask of tragedy, and then she laid it against her husband's shoulder again and cried even harder.

'Mildred, please stop. The doctor told us he didn't think it would be anything much. He told us that, didn't he? I said to him that we had to know the worst, but he said there wasn't any worst. You'd be out in a week, he said . . .' He went on talking like this in a soothing firm voice, and stroked her, and made concerned noises, and she burst out in worse sobs and clung and then shook her head to say she wasn't crying about her medical treatment, but for reasons he knew about yet wilfully chose to ignore.

So noisy were her tears that a nurse came in and stood staring, but did not know what to do. The husband, Tom, looked gravely at the nurse. This was not a helpless look, far from it: rather, he was saying, There's no more I can do and now it's your job.

'Mildred, I am going now.' And he disengaged himself, pulling down her arms which instantly flew up again around his neck. He finally got free, laid her back on her pillows, stood up, and said genially (not apologetically, for this was not a man who would easily see a need for apologies, but giving an explanation they were entitled to have), 'You see, my wife and I have never been separated, not even for one night, not since we were married, not for twenty-five years.' Hearing this his wife nodded frantically while the tears rained down all over her pretty pink jacket. Then, seeing him stand upright there, refusing to bend down to her again, she turned her gaze away from him and stared at the wall.

'I'm going now, dear,' said Tom, and went out, giving the nurse a look that silently commanded her to take over.

'Well now, Mrs Grant,' said the nurse in the cheerful voice of her discipline. She was a girl of about twenty, and she looked tired, and the last thing she needed was an old woman (as she would see it) complaining and carrying on. 'You're disturbing all the others, you mustn't be selfish,' she attempted, hopefully.

The appeal had no effect, as the ironical faces of the other women showed they had expected. But Mildred Grant was crying less noisily now. 'Would you like a nice cup of tea?' No reply. Only gasps and little sniffs. The nurse looked at the others who were all so much older than she was, and went out.

Nine o'clock. Soon they would be expected to sleep. In came a trolley with milky drinks of a sleep-inducing kind. Some of the women were brushing their hair, or putting in rollers, or rubbing cream methodically into their necks and faces. There was a feeling of lull, of marking time: the day shift had gone home and the night staff were coming on.

The old woman – the really old woman, whom the nurses called Granny – remarked brightly, 'My husband died twenty years ago. I've lived by myself for twenty years. We were happy, we were. But I've been alone since he died.'

The crying stopped. One or two of the women sent congratulatory smiles and grimaces to the speaker, but then there was a fresh outburst from the abandoned wife.

A sigh from the old woman, a shrug. 'Some people don't know their luck,' she said.

'No, they don't,' said the woman opposite her, Miss Cook. 'I've never had a husband at all. Every time I thought I 'ad one nice and hooked, he wriggled away!' She laughed loudly, as she had often done at this brave joke, and glanced quickly at the others to make sure she had made her effect. They were laughing. Miss Cook was a comic. Probably it was this very joke that had set her off on her career of being one, decades ago. She was a large, formidable, red-faced woman of about seventy.

Soon they were all washed, brushed, tidy, and in bed. The night nurse, another fresh young woman, came to look them over. She had heard from the nurses going off duty about the difficult patient, and now she gave the sobbing Mildred Grant a long, dubious inspection, and said, 'Good night, ladies, good night.' She seemed as if she might try admonitions or advice, but went out, switching off the light.

It was not dark in the room. The tall yellow lamps that illuminated the hospital car park shone in here. There was a pattern of light and dark on the walls, and the pink of the curtains showed, a subdued but brave note.

Seven women lay tense in their beds, listening to Mildred Grant.

Her bed was near the door. In the two beds beside hers were matrons in the full energies of middle age, who commanded children, daughters-in-law, sons-in-law, husbands, relatives of all kinds, and these were always dropping in with flowers and fruit in what seemed to the others like a continuing family party. Mrs Joan Lee and Mrs Rosemary Stamford demanded the movable telephones several times a day to organize dentists' and doctors' appointments, to remind their families of this or that, or to ring up grocers' or greengrocers' shops to order food the happy-go-lucky ones at home were bound to forget. They might be in the hospital with womb

problems, but in spirit they had hardly been here at all.
Now they were forced to be here, to listen. The fourth bed
on that side held the joker, Miss Cook. Opposite her was
the very old woman, the widow. Beside her, 'the horsey
one', a handsome young woman with the high, clear,
commanding voice of her class, who was neither chummy
nor standoffish, defended a stubborn privacy with books
and her Walkman. Atavistic dislikes had caused the others
to agree (when she was out of the room) that her abortion
on the National Health was selfish: she should have gone
to a private hospital, for with those clothes and general
style she could certainly afford to. Next to her a recently
married girl who had miscarried lay limp in her bed, like
a drowned girl, pale and sad but brave. Next to her and
opposite Mildred Grant was a dancer, no longer young,
and so now she had to teach others how to dance. She
had fallen and as a result suffered internal hurt. She was
depressed but putting a good face on it. 'Laugh and the
world laughs with you!' she often cried, full of vivacity.
This was her motto, and, too, 'It's a great life if you don't
weaken!'

The women were shifting about in their beds. Their eyes
shone in the lights from the car park. An hour passed. The
night nurse heard the sound of weeping from outside, and
came in. She stood by the bed and said, 'Mrs Grant, what
are you doing? My patients have to get some sleep. And
you should, too. You're going to have an examination in
the morning. There's nothing to be afraid of, but you
should be rested.'

The sobbing continued.

'Well, I don't know,' said the nurse. 'If she doesn't stop
in a few minutes, ring the bell.' And she went out.

Mildred Grant was now crying more softly. It was a
dreary automatic sobbing and by now it was badly on
their nerves. In every one of them dwelled the unappeased

child with her rights and her claims, and they were being forced to remember her, and how much it had cost them all to subdue her. The pale girl who had miscarried was weeping. Silently, but they saw the tears glisten on her cheeks. The gallant dancer lay curled in a foetal position, her thumb in her mouth. The 'horsey one' – she, in fact, loathed horses – had slipped the Walkman's earpieces back on, but she was watching, and probably unable to stop herself listening through whatever sounds she had chosen to shut out the noise of weeping. The women were all aware of each other, watched each other, afraid that one of them would really crack and even begin screaming.

Mrs Rosemary Stamford, a tough matron, the last person you'd think would give way, said in a peevish end-of-my-tether voice, 'They should move her into another ward. It's not fair. I'm going to talk to them.'

But before she could move, Miss Cook was getting out of her bed. She was not only large and unwieldy but full of rheumatism, and it took time. Then, slowly, she put on a flowered dressing gown, padded because she said her room was cold and she couldn't afford what was needed to keep it heated, and bent to pull on her slippers. Was she going out to appeal to the nurses? To the toilet? At any rate, watching her took their minds off Mildred Grant.

It was to Mildred Grant she went. She settled herself in the chair that had been occupied for all those hours by the husband, and laid a firm hand on Mildred's shoulder.

'Now then, love,' she said, or commanded. 'I want you to listen to me. Are you listening? We are all in the same boat here. We've got our little troubles, we have, all of us. I had to have a hysteriaectomy' – so she pronounced it, as a joke, for while she was a real old-style working-class woman, unlike the others here except for the widow, she knew quite well how the word should be said. 'The way I see it, it's not fair. What's my womb ever done for me?'

Here she raised her face so the others could see that she
was closing her left eye in a wink. Always good for a laugh,
that's me, said this wink. Now she said loudly, to be heard
over the sobbing, 'Look, dear, if you've had someone to
say goodnight to every night of your life, then it's more
than most people have. Can't you see it like that?'

Mildred went on crying.

They could all see Miss Cook's face in the light from
the window. It looked strained and tired, the jolly clown
notwithstanding.

She laid her arm around the weeping woman's shoulders and gently shook her. 'Now, my dear,' she said, 'don't
cry like that, you really mustn't . . .'

But Mildred had turned and flung her arms around Miss
Cook's neck. 'Oh,' she wept. 'I'm sorry, but I can't help it.
I've never had to sleep by myself, not ever, I've always had
my Tom . . .'

Miss Cook put her arms right around Mildred, cradling
and rocking the poor bereft little girl. Her face was, as they
say, a study. She seemed to be struggling with herself.
When at last she spoke, her voice was rough, even angry.
'What a lucky girl you are, aren't you? Always had Tom,
'ave you? And I'm sure a lot of us wish we could say the
same.' Then she checked her anger and began again in a
soothing monotonous tone. 'Poor little thing, poor little
girl, what a shame, is that what it is, then, oh dear, poor
thing . . .'

· The other women were remembering that Miss Cook
had not had children, had never been married, and lived
alone, and apart from her cat had no one to touch, stroke,
hold. And here she was, her arms filled with Mildred
Grant, and probably this was the first time in years
she had had her arms around another person, man or
woman.

What must it feel like, being reminded of this other

world where people hugged and held and kissed and
lay close at night, and woke in the dark out of a dream
to feel arms around them, or were able to reach out and
say, 'Hold me, I've been dreaming'?

But her voice was going on, kindly, impersonal, firm.
'Poor little thing. Poor little girl. What a shame, but never
mind, you'll have your Tom back soon, won't you . . .'

This went on for a good quarter of an hour. The sobbing
stopped. Miss Cook laid down the exhausted woman,
letting her limbs and head flop gently into a comfortable
position, as one does with a child.

When she stood up and looked down at the sleeping
woman, Miss Cook's face was, if possible, even more of
a study. She went to her bed, removed her flowery gown
and her slippers and lay carefully down.

The women communicated without words.

It was necessary for someone to say something. It was
she, Miss Cook, who had to say it. 'Well,' she remarked.
'You live and learn.'

Soon they were all in their own worlds, fast asleep.

Principles

I was driving up one of the roads in Hampstead which, as we all know, were never designed for cars, were not long ago lanes that accommodated horses and people walking. In front of me a knot in the traffic. Hardly unusual. I stopped. I had to. In front of me was a Golf, and in front of that a blue Escort was blocked by a red van, nose to nose. If the red van reversed no more than a couple of yards, then the Escort could drive past. But the red van wasn't going to budge, although for the Escort to let him through meant that the woman – yes, yes, a woman driver – would have to reverse past a parked car and then abruptly at an angle into an empty space too small for it, so it would stick out anyway. If the Escort did this, yes, there would be room for the red van to go past, but only just. The sensible thing was for the red van to reverse.

It was evident that this was a question of Principle. Principle was what we were up against. The red van was faced with a woman driver who wouldn't give way. The Escort was faced with an unreasonable bully of a man. The woman driver was damned if she was going to go through this ridiculous business of reversing and then going sharply back into a silly space that wouldn't even hold the Escort, when for the van to reverse would be the work of seconds.

There were cars on the other side of the red van, a line stretching all the way up the hill.

They hooted. The Golf in front of me hooted to keep them company. Then the man in the Golf got out and walked to where he could stand by the window of the Escort and talk to the woman, and after that he went to the window of the red van.

He turned and slowly came back. He had decided to find it entertaining. His face was all resigned, amused philosophy. He was waggling his hands, palms down, on either side of his thighs in the way that says, 'Here we have a pretty kettle of fish! However, let's keep calm.' He shrugged and got into his car. Then he stuck out his head and signalled to me to reverse. Just behind me on my left was a street going off up a hill, but a girl in a Toyota blocked the way. She was in trouble with a lorry, behind her. The man in the lorry was shouting that everything was the fault of the woman driver up in front, but the Toyota girl wasn't going to have that. She said nothing, but sat smiling, a tight angry little smile. The man in the lorry jumped down, shook his fist at the Toyota, then – for good measure – at me, and strode smartly up past us both and past the Golf, and reached the two vehicles standing nose to nose. He had not been able to see from the cab of the lorry that the red van – male – was more in the wrong than the Escort. He shouted a little at the woman in the Escort, just for the look of the thing. She was now smoking so energetically that it seemed the driver's seat was on fire. He did not bother to speak to the driver of the red van, from which one could deduce that he could see it would do no good. He came back, not looking at the man in the Golf who – he could now see – was not going to be an ally, but probably regarded him as at fault, then

past me, then past the girl in the Toyota. He climbed back
into his cab and looked to see how he could reverse to let
the Toyota go out left. But behind him now were several
cars. He shouted at them to reverse, and while we couldn't
see them it was evident they were furious too, because
they were hooting. At last he was able to reverse a short
way. Then the woman in the Toyota began complicated
to-ings and fro-ings to get herself out into the leftwards
street. Then she had gone, and I wanted to reverse, but
the lorry had already come forward. This made the Golf
in front of me start a frenzied hooting. He shouted at the
lorry to go out left. But the lorry wasn't going to leave the
scene, because one or other of the two contenders for being
proved in the right of it ought to give way, and he was
going to wait until he, or she, did. Now this man tried to
reverse again, to let me and the Golf out, but meanwhile
other hooting cars had pressed up behind him. It took
time for him to slowly press back and back so that I could
reverse, and go off into the side street. The man in the
Golf reversed the very second he could, which meant he
was going slowly back towards the lorry that was coming
slowly forwards. As I left the scene the two were shouting
at each other.

I drove up the street. You can, if you want, turn so
as to rejoin the street I had just extricated myself from.
Why did I decide to do this? The spirit of obstinacy had
entered me too. Besides, I didn't *see* why I had to drive
half a mile out of my way. In short, no, there's no excuse. I
rejoined the street about twenty yards past where the red
van stood obstinately in front of the Escort. Now I could
see the face, or rather, the profile of the driver of the red
van. He was elderly, overweight, and his cheek looked
as if it had been washed in the water beetroot had been
boiled in. A candidate for a stroke. Out of the window of
the Escort billowed smoke. I could just see her face: the

strong features of a woman who would stand to the death for common sense and her rights.

Behind the red van the long line of blocked cars was trying to dissolve itself by backing up the hill and then turning off right into the street parallel to the one I had come from. That meant that I and the cars behind me, including the Golf, had to wait while all these cars reversed and manoeuvred. All the time cars were adding themselves to this line, and hooting, and people were shouting at each other, because they had not understood the seriousness of the situation with the red van and the Escort. The man in the Golf, the one who had waggled his hands in a gesture of world-weary tolerance, could not see what was holding me up now. He leant out and shouted at me and I leant out and shouted that there were about fifteen cars ahead sorting themselves out. He finally cracked. He yelled, 'Oh Christ, would you believe it!' and gestured to the cars behind him that he was going to reverse. There was just room, and he went forward into the drive of a man who came out of the house to shout that his drive was not a public roadway.

A woman from the manoeuvring cars behind the red van held them all up to walk down to the red van and the Escort, where she surveyed the scene, and then said to the puce-faced driver and the smoke-shrouded woman, 'Well, I suppose you two are getting something out of all this.'

And went back to her car.

At last I was able to go fast enough ahead to get a place going up the hill before yet another car turned in front of me. At the top of the hill I slowed to look around and there was the red van, there was the Escort, and neither had conceded an inch.

D.H.S.S.

The young woman on the pavement's edge was facing in, not out to the street, and she moved about there indecisively, but with a stubborn look. Several times she seemed about to approach somebody who had just come out of the Underground to walk up the street, but then she stopped and retreated. At last she moved in to block the advance of a smartly dressed matron with a toy dog on a leash that came to sniff around her legs as she said hurriedly, 'Please give me some money. I've got to have it. The Social Security's on strike and I've got to feed my kids.' Resentment made her stumble over her words. The woman examined her, nodded, took a £5 note from her handbag, then put it back and chose a £10 note. She handed it over. The young woman stood with it in her hand, looking at it disbelievingly. She muttered a reluctant 'Thanks', and at once turned and crossed the street in a blind, determined way, holding up one hand to halt the traffic. She was going to the supermarket opposite the Underground station, but at the entrance stopped to glance back at the woman who had given her the money. She was standing there watching her, the little dog yapping and bouncing at the end of its leash. 'Fucking cheek. Checking to see if I was lying,' muttered the young woman. But she was a girl, really. 'I'll kill her. I'll kill them . . .' And she went in, took a basket, and began selecting bread, margarine, peanut butter, cans of soup.

This incident had been observed by a man sitting in a shabby blue Datsun at the pavement's edge. He had got out of the car and crossed the street just behind her, holding up his hand against the traffic to support her. He followed her in to the supermarket. He was a few paces behind her during her progress through the shop. At the check-out desk, when she took out the £10 note, her face tense with the anxiety of wondering if it would be enough, he interposed his own £10 note, forcing it into the check-out girl's hand. By the time the girl he had been following understood what he was doing it was too late. 'OK,' he said, 'let's fight outside.' She looked angrily at him, and at the check-out girl, who was already busy with the next customer. Then she followed him to the pavement. She was not looking at him to find what he was like, but how to quarrel with him. In fact he was a man of perhaps forty, with nothing particular about him, and dressed as casually as she was. But he had all the carelessness of confidence. Her clothes were ordinary, that is to say jeans and a sweater, but she had a drab appearance, not so much dirty as stale. Her hands were nicotine-stained.

'Look,' he said, taking all this in, 'I know what you want to say, but why don't we have a cup of coffee?'

She just stood there. She was frozen . . . it was with suspicion. She looked trapped. A few yards away a couple of tables with chairs around them stood outside a café.

'Come on,' said he, with a jerk of his head towards the tables. He sat down at one, and she did too, in a helpless, lethargic way, but as if she was about to leap up again. At once she started peering into the carrier bags for just-bought cigarettes. She lit a cigarette and sat with her eyes closed, and smoked as if trying to drown in smoke, pulling breaths of it deep into her lungs. He said, 'I'm going to order. Coffee?' No movement from her. 'I'll get coffee then. And I know you are hungry. What do you want to eat?' No response. She went on drawing in smoke from the cigarette held to her lips in a childish grubby hand.

He went into the café. His quick glance back showed he was afraid she would be off. But when he came back with two cups of coffee she had not moved. He sat down, putting the cups on the table, and she at once pulled one towards her, piled in sugar and drank it in big gulps. Before she had finished it, he went back in and returned with another cup which he put down before her.

'Don't think you're going to get something out of this because you won't,' she said angrily.

'I know that,' he said, in a voice kept reasonable. He was sorry for her and could not keep this out of his face and eyes. But she had not once looked at him properly.

There arrived before them a large plate of sandwiches.

'Go on, eat,' he said.

She took up a sandwich without enthusiasm, sat with it in her hand, and at last did look at him. A rapid once-over, expecting the worst: her face seemed forever set in sarcastic rage.

'Well, then, what's all this for?' she asked, cold.

'I used to work in a D.H.S.S. office,' he said, as if it were an explanation. Her face – if this was possible – got even harder and angrier. Her eyes narrowed and shot out beams of hate. 'Yes, yes,' he said, 'I know what you want to say.'

'No you don't. You don't know anything about me.'

'I'm making a fair old guess,' he said, with deliberate humour, but she wasn't going to have that.

'You don't know a bloody thing about me and you're not going to.'

'I know you haven't got the money to feed your kids.'

'How do you know I've got kids?'

He smiled, mildly impatient. 'I wouldn't have to be Sherlock Holmes. And I'm sure you wouldn't be begging if you didn't need it for your kids.'

This froze her up. She had not known, it seemed, that she had been observed begging. Then she decided not to care. She crammed in a big bite of the sandwich, holding her cigarette at the ready in the other hand. 'I suppose you're full of remorse about being on strike,' she jeered, as soon as her mouth was empty.

'I told you, I used to work there. I don't now. I left a year ago. I left because I couldn't stand it.'

It was evident he needed to go on telling her, but she shook her head to say she wasn't interested.

'I'd like to kill them,' she said, meaning it. 'I would if I could. What do they think . . . they *don't* think. I haven't been able to collect any money for three weeks and it was their mistake in the first place, not mine. And now they're on strike. They owe me a full month. I haven't paid my rent. I borrowed money from someone who doesn't have any either. Then they go on strike for a rise . . . they don't care about us, they never think about what is happening to us. I could kill them.'

He said uncomfortably, his eyes bright with sympathy for her, 'Look at it from their point of view . . .'

'What point of view?' she cut in. 'I'm only interested in my point of view. I had a friend downstairs, she killed herself last time they decided to treat themselves to going on strike. She had two kids. They're in care now. I got myself a job a couple of months ago. It wasn't much of a job but it was a job. But hanging around Social Security day after day to try and get my money out of them, I lost it. Now I haven't even got that. I'm not going to try for another job, what's the point? If I did get one, the shitting

D.H.S.S. would decide to go on strike again.' She delivered all this in a cold level tone, her eyes – the vulnerable eyes of a girl – staring off at nothing. She was probably seeing visions of herself killing enemies.

He said, sounding discouraged, 'Not everyone in the Social Security agrees with the strike. I'm sure of that.'

'I don't care. Well, I've come to begging. I did it last time they went on strike. I shoplifted too. If I hadn't, the kids'd've starved.'

'How many have you got?'

'What's it to you? I'm not telling you anything.'

He leaned forward, peering into the cloud of smoke she sat in, and said, speaking slowly and deliberately, to make her listen to him, 'When I started working there it was all different. Fifteen years ago . . . I really liked it then, I liked . . .' Here he censored 'helping people', but she heard it and gave him a sour smile. 'But then everything slowly went to pot. In those days there was a good atmosphere, not like it is now. We were understaffed suddenly. Then the cuts . . . suddenly they put up partitions and glass panels and bars in the windows. We were shut off from – the customers, so to speak. It was like being in a cage. Not that I wasn't sometimes glad of the protection.' He laughed: it sounded like grudging admiration. He held out his arm and pulled back the sleeve of his jacket, showing a reddened lump just above his wrist. 'See that? That's where a girl bit me. She went berserk . . .'

'Probably me,' she said, not looking at him. Her pose said she didn't want to listen to all this. His attitude said that he had to say it: he was full of the need to tell her.

'No, it wasn't you. I'll never forget that girl.'

'Could have been, though.'

'Then you'd have been in the wrong of it. That time it wasn't our fault. She got herself in a muddle and blamed us.'

'If you say so. If you say something then it has to be true. No appeal. Going berserk, is that what you call it?' She was stubbing out a cigarette and wondering whether to light another. She looked at her watch: yes, she had a bit more time.

He said, 'Ten quid's worth of food isn't going to get you very far.'

'I've got the ten that rich cow gave me.'

He took out his wallet, extracted a £10 note, then a £5 note, and handed them to her. 'Go into the shop again. Stock up a bit.'

She looked at the money in her hand, her mouth ugly. She got up, then remembered the carrier bags on the chair beside her, and was about to take them into the shop with her.

'Do you think I'm going to steal them?' He sounded hurt, but she only shrugged, and went into the supermarket. While she was gone he allowed his face to show what he was feeling: anger, but it was different from hers, and he did not seem able to believe what he was remembering, what he was thinking. He was full of frustration.

When she came back laden he was smiling. She could hardly walk as she returned to the table. He said, 'Sit down, finish your sandwiches.'

She considered this on its merits. She sat. And ate up the sandwiches slowly, methodically, without appetite.

He watched her. He said, 'I've been driving a mini-cab for a year now. I don't earn what I did, but we manage.'

No response. She had lit another cigarette.

'I've got a wife and two kids,' he said.

'Good for them.'

'If you want to put that stuff in my car I'll run you home.'

'What sort of a fool do you take me for? For £25 and some coffee and sandwiches you'd know where I live.'

Now he sat silenced.

She glanced up because he had not replied, saw his face, and said, 'No I *don't* trust anyone. And I never will again.'

'You're going to stagger home with all that stuff rather than trust me?'

'That's right.' She stood, and hoisted up the bags. One held twenty pounds of potatoes.

He got up too. 'If you put that stuff in my car I'll run you somewhere near where you live. You can tell me where to stop. It'll cut down the distance a bit.'

'I don't know why you're doing this. And I don't care. I don't give a fuck.'

'All right,' he said patiently, though he sounded fed up. 'I didn't ask you to care. I made you an offer. Anyway, don't be so bloody stupid. If I wanted to find out where you live all I'd have to do is hang around the schools in the area. It's probably Fortescue, isn't it?' He was going on, but stopped, because of her face.

'All right,' she said, not looking at him.

He took a couple of the carriers from her, and went across the road in front of her, holding up his hand to slow a car. She followed. She got into the back seat. He put the carriers in beside her. He got into the front seat and said, 'Where to?'

'Just drive down this street.'

After about a mile, near Kentish Town, she said, 'This'll do.'

He stopped the car. She got out. He was gazing in front of him, not at her.

She said, and it killed her to say it, 'Thanks.'

'Don't mention it,' he said.

He sat on there, watching her go slowly along the

pavement, her shoulders pulled down with the weight of the bags. She turned into a street he knew she did not live in. He was waiting to see if she would turn and wave or smile or even just look at him, but she did not.

Casualty

All of them looking one way, they sat on metal chairs, the kind that are hard and slippery and stack into each other. They kept their attention on the woman behind the reception desk, who was apparently not interested in them now she had their names, addresses, complaints all tidily written down on forms. She was an ample young woman with the rainy violet eyes that seem designed only for laughing or weeping, but now they were full of the stern impartiality of justice. Her name button said she was Nurse Doolan.

It was a large room with walls an uninteresting shade of beige, bare except for the notice, 'If You Have Nothing Urgently Wrong Please Go To Your Own Doctor'. Evidently the twenty or so people here did not believe their own doctors were as good as this hospital casualty department. Only one of them seemed in urgent need, a dishevelled woman of forty or so with dyed orange hair, who was propping her wrapped left hand on her right shoulder. Everyone knew the wrist was broken because the woman with her had nodded commandingly at them, turning round to do it, and mouthed, 'Her *wrist*. She broke it.' Satisfied they must all acknowledge precedence, she had placed her charge in the end of the front row nearest to the door that said 'No Admittance'. They did not challenge her. The broken-wristed one, exhausted with pain, drowsed in her seat, and her face was bluish white, so that with the brush of orange hair she looked like a clown. But Nurse Doolan did not seem to think she deserved more than the others, for when the next name was called it was not the owner of the wrist. 'Harkness,' said Nurse Doolan and while an apparently fit young man walked into 'No Admittance' the poor clown's attendant stood up and complained, 'But it is urgent, it is a broken *wrist*.'

'Won't be long,' said Nurse Doolan, and placidly studied her pile of forms.

'They don't care. They don't care at all,' said an old woman in a wheelchair. Her voice was loud and accusing. She was fat and looked like a constipated frog. Her face, full of healthy colour, showed a practised resignation to life's taunts. 'I fell down a good six hours ago, and my shoulder's broke, I know that!' The elderly woman sitting with her did not try to engage anyone's sympathy, but rather avoided eyes that had already clearly said, Rather you than me! She said quietly, 'It's all right, Auntie, don't go on.'

'Don't go on, *she* says,' said the old woman, eighty if she was a day, and full of energy. 'It's all right for some.'

A boy of about twelve emerged from the mysteries behind 'No Admittance' with a crutch and a bandaged foot, and was guided through this waiting room to the outside pavement by a nurse who left him there, presumably to be picked up. She came back.

'Nurse,' said the old woman, 'my shoulder's broke and I've been sitting here for hours ... ever so long,' she added, as her relative murmured, 'Not long, Auntie, only half an hour.'

This nurse glanced towards Doolan at Reception, who

signalled with her violet eyes. Nurse Bates, directed, stopped by the wheelchair and switched on appropriate sympathy. 'Let's have a look,' she said. The elderly niece drew back part of a bright pink cardigan from the shoulder which sat there, stoutly and soberly bare, except for a grimy shoulder strap. 'You want me naked, I suppose that's it now! For everyone to gape at! That's it, I suppose!' The nurse bent over the shoulder, gently manipulating it, while everybody stared somewhere else, so as not to give the old horror the satisfaction of feeling looked at.

'Owwwww,' wailed the old woman.

'You'll live,' said the nurse briskly, straightening herself.

'It's broken, isn't it?' urged Auntie.

'You've got a bit of a bruise, but that's about it, I think. They'll find out in X-ray.' And she stepped smartly off towards 'No Admittance', raising her brows and smiling with her eyes at Nurse Doolan, who smiled with hers.

'They don't care,' came the loud voice. 'None of them care. How'd you like to be lying on the floor by yourself half the night and no one near you to lift you up?'

The elderly niece, a thin and colourless creature who probably – though for her sake everyone hoped not – devoted her life to this old bully, did not bother to defend herself, but smoothed back the pink cardigan over the shoulder which if you looked hard did have a mauveish shine.

'Day after day, sitting by myself, I might as well be dead.'

'Would you like a cup of tea, Auntie?'

'Might as well, if you'll put yourself out. Not that it'll be worth drinking.'

The niece allowed her face to show a moment's exhaustion as she turned away from Auntie, but then she smiled and went through the rows of waiting people with 'Excuse me, excuse me, please'.

'Fanshawe,' said Nurse Doolan, apparently in reply to some summons in the ether, for no one had come out.

A man of sixty-five or so, who wore a red leather slipper on one foot, used a stick to heave himself up, and walked slowly to the inner door, careful the stick did not slip.

'You'd think they'd have nonslip floors,' came from the wheelchair.

'They *are* nonslip,' said Doolan firmly.

'Better be safe than sorry,' said Mr Fanshawe going into 'No Admittance' with a wink all round that meant he wasn't going to be associated with that old bitch.

'And what about my sister?' asked the woman who was now cradling the broken-wristed one. Her voice trembled, and she seemed about to weep with indignation.

And indeed the poor clown seemed half conscious, her orange head drooping, then jerking up, then falling forward, and she even groaned. She heard herself groan and embarrassment woke her up. She flashed painful smiles along the front row, and as far as she could turn her head to the back. 'I fell,' she muttered, confessing it, begging forgiveness. 'I fell, you see.'

'You're not the only one to fall,' came from the wheelchair.

'There's been a bad accident,' said Nurse Doolan. 'They've been working in there like navvies these last three hours.'

'Oh, that's it, is it?' 'That's what it is, then!' 'Oh well, in that case . . .' came from the longsuffering crowd.

'Never seen anything like it,' said Nurse Doolan, sharing this with them.

It was noticeable that she and some others glanced nervously at the old woman, who decided not to have her say, not this time. And here was her niece with her tea in the plastic foam cup.

'And what did I tell you?' demanded Auntie, taking the cup and at once noisily gulping the tea. 'Plastic rubbish and it's cold, you'd think . . .'

A trundling sound from inside 'No Admittance'. As the doors opened there emerged the back of a young black porter in his natty uniform, then a steel trolley, and on the trolley a human form rolled in bandages to the waist, but naked above and showing a strong healthy young man's chest. Black. From the neck began a cocoon: a white bandaged head. Alert brown eyes looked out from the cocoon. The trolley disappeared into the interior of the hospital on its way to some ward several floors up.

'The wrist,' said Nurse Doolan, 'Bisley,' and the woman with the broken wrist was urged to her feet by her sister, and stood swaying. Doolan at once pressed a bell which they heard shrilling inside 'No Admittance'. The same nurse came running out, saw why she had been summoned, and with Nurse Bates on one side and her sister on the other the half-conscious Wrist was supported within.

Now a new addition to the morning's casualties. In came two young women, made up and dressed up as if off to a disco, chattering away and apparently in the best of health. They lowered their voices, sensing that their jollity was not being appreciated, and sat at the very back, whispering and sometimes giggling. What could they be doing in Casualty?

It seemed that at any moment this was what the old woman would start asking, for she was fixing them with a hard, cold, accusing look. 'Auntie,' said her niece hastily, 'would you like another tea? I could do with one myself.'

'I don't mind.' And she graciously handed over her cup. The niece went out again.

And then, everything changed. A group of young men appeared outside the glass doors to the world where cars came and went, where visitors walked past, where there was ordinariness and health. This group sent waves of urgency and alarm into the waiting room even before the doors opened.

A young workman in white overalls blotched with red stood gripping the edge of a door because over his shoulder lay a body, and it was heavy, as they could all see, being limp and with no fight in it. This body was a young man too, but his white overalls were soaked with a dreadful dark pulsing blood that still welled from somewhere.

'Why didn't you . . .' began Nurse Doolan, on her way to saying, 'You're not supposed to come in at that door, you need a stretcher, this isn't at all how we do things . . .' Something on these lines, but no one would ever know, for having taken one look at what was before them, she put her thumb down on the bell to make it shrill in the ears of the doctors and nurses working inside out of sight.

Feet and voices, and out came running the same nurse; three doctors – two women and a man – and a porter with a stretcher.

Seeing the group of young men just inside the door these professionals all stopped still, and the main woman doctor waved aside the stretcher.

'He fell off the roof,' said the young man who held his mate. 'He fell off.' He sounded incredulous, appealing to them, the experts, to say that this was impossible and could not have happened. His mate at his elbow, a youth whose sky-blue overalls had no spot or stain, corroborated, 'Yes, he fell off. Suddenly he wasn't there. And then . . .' Another youth, following behind, still held a paint roller in one hand. Orange paint. These three young men were about twenty, certainly not more than twenty-two or twenty-three. They were pale, shocked, and their eyes told everyone they had seen something terrible and could not stop looking at it.

The woman doctor in charge summoned the group forward, and the doctors and nurse stood to one side as the young men went through into 'No Admittance'. Blood pattered down.

And then they were all able to see the face that hung over the blood-soaked shoulder. It was dull grey, not a colour many of them were likely to have seen on a face. The mouth hung open. The eyes were open. Blue eyes . . . The professionals followed the young men in, and the doors swung shut.

Nurse Doolan came out from behind the desk with a cloth, and bent to wipe blood off the floor. She too looked sick.

Meanwhile the second cup of tea arrived, and the old woman took it. The niece, feeling that something had happened in the few minutes she had been gone, was looking around, but no one looked at her. They stared at 'No Admittance', and their faces were full of news.

'Well,' said the old woman loudly, full of gleeful energy. 'I haven't done badly at that, have I? I am eighty-five this year and there's plenty more where that came from!'

No one looked at her, and no one said anything.

In Defence of the Underground

In a small cigarette and sweet shop outside the Underground station, the Indian behind the counter is in energetic conversation with a young man. They are both so angry that customers thinking of coming in change their minds.

'They did my car in, they drove past so near they scraped all the paint off that side. I saw them do it. I was at my window – just luck, that was. They were laughing like dogs. Then they turned around and drove back and scraped the paint off the other side. They went off like bats out of hell. They saw me at the window and laughed.'

'You're going to have to take it into your own hands,' says the Indian. 'They did up my brother's shop last month. They put burning paper through the letter box. It was luck the whole shop didn't burn. The police didn't do anything. He rang them, and then he went round to the station. Nothing doing. So we found out where they lived and we went and smashed their car in.'

'Yes,' says the other, who is a white man, not an Indian. 'The police don't want to know. I told them. I saw them do it. They were drunk, I said. What do you expect us to do? the police said.'

'I'll tell you what you can do,' says the Indian.

All this time I stand there, disregarded. They are too angry to care who hears them and, it follows, might report them. Then the young white man says – he could be something in building, or a driver, 'You think I should do the same, then?'

'You take a good sized hammer or a crowbar to their car, if you know where they live.'

'I've a fair old idea, yes.'

'Then that's it.'

'Right, that's it.' And he goes out, though he has to return for the cigarettes he came to buy, for in his rage he has forgotten them.

The Indian serves me. He is on automatic, his hands at work, his mind elsewhere.

As I go out, 'Cheers,' he says, and then, continuing the other conversation, 'That's it, then.'

In our area the Indian shop-keepers defend their shops at night with close-meshed grills, like chain mail – and it is not only the Indian shops.

Now I am standing on the pavement in a garden. It is a pavement garden, for the florist puts her plants out here, disciplined ranks of them, but hopeful plants, aspiring, because it is bedding plant time, in other words, late spring. A lily flowering a good month early scents the air stronger than the stinks of the traffic that pounds up this main route north all day and half the night. It is an ugly road, one you avoid if in a car, for one may need half an hour to go a few hundred yards.

Not long ago just where I stand marked the end of London. I know this because an old woman told me she used to take a penny bus here from Marble Arch, every Sunday. That is, she did, 'If I had a penny to spare, I used to save up from my dinners, I used to look forward all week. It was all fields and little streams, and we took

off our shoes and stockings and sat with our feet in the
water and looked at the cows. They used to come and look
at us. And the birds – there were plenty of those.' That
was before the First World War, in that period described
in books of memoirs as a Golden Age. Yet you can find
on stationers' counters postcards made from photographs
of this street a hundred years or so ago. It has never not
been a poor street, and it is a poor one now, even in this
particular age of Peace and Plenty. Not much has changed,
though shop fronts are flashier, and full of bright cheap
clothes, and there is a petrol station. The postcards show
modest self-regarding buildings and the ground floor of
every one is a shop of a kind long since extinct, where
each customer was served individually. Outside them,
invited from behind a counter to centre the picture, stand
men in bowler hats or serving aprons; if it is a woman
she has a hat on of the kind that insisted on obdurate
respectability, for that is a necessary attribute of the poor.
But only a couple of hundred yards north-west my friend
sat on Sundays with her feet in the little streams, while
the cows crowded close. 'Oh, it was so cold, the water'd
take your breath away, but you'd soon forget that, and it
was the best day of the week.' A few hundred yards north
there used to be a mill. Another woman, younger than the
first, told me she remembered the Mill. 'Mill Lane – the
name's because there used to be a mill, you see. But they
pulled the mill down.' And where it was is a building no
one would notice, if you didn't know what it replaced.
If they had let the mill stand we would be proud of it,
and they would charge us to go in and see how things
used to be.

I enter the station, buy a ticket from a machine that
works most of the time, and go up long stairs. There
used to be decent lavatories, but now they are locked up
because they are vandalized as soon as repaired. There is

a good waiting room with heating, but often a window is smashed, and there is always graffiti. What are the young people saying when they smash everything they can? – for it is young people who do it, usually men. It is not that they are depraved because they are deprived, for I have just visited a famous university up north, where they have twenty applications for every place, where ninety-nine per cent of the graduates get jobs within a year of leaving. These are the privileged young, and they make for themselves a lively and ingenious social life their teachers clearly admire, if not envy. Yet they too smash everything up, not just the usual undergraduate loutishness, boys will be boys, but what seems to be a need for systematic destruction. What need? Do we know?

At the station you stand to wait for trains on a platform high above roofs and the tree tops are level with you. You feel thrust up into the sky. The sun, the wind, the rain, arrive unmediated by buildings. Exhilarating.

I like travelling by Underground. This is a defiant admission. I am always hearing, reading, I hate the Underground. In a book I have just picked up the author says he seldom uses it, but when he did have to go a few stops, he found it disgusting. A strong word. If people have to travel in the rush hour, then all is understood, but you may hear people who know nothing about rush hours say how terrible the Underground is. This is the Jubilee Line and I use it all the time. Fifteen minutes at the most to get in to the centre. The carriages are bright and new – well, almost. There are efficient indicators, Charing Cross: five minutes, three minutes, one minute. The platforms are no more littered than the streets, often less, or not at all. 'Ah but you should have seen what they were like in the old days. The Tube was different then.'

I know an old woman, I am sure I should say lady, who says, 'People like you . . .' She means aliens, foreigners, though I have lived here forty years . . . 'have no idea what London was like. You could travel from one side of London to the other by taxi for half a crown.' (In Elizabeth I's time you could buy a sheep for a few pence and under the Romans doubtless you could buy a villa for a silver coin, but currencies never devaluate when Nostalgia is in this gear.) 'And everything was so nice and clean and people were polite. Buses were always on time and the Tube was cheap.'

This woman was one of London's Bright Young Things, her young time was the twenties. As she speaks her face is tenderly reminiscent, but lonely, and she does not expect to persuade me or anyone else. What is the point of having lived in that Paradise Isle if no one believes you? As she sings her praise-songs for the past one sees hosts of pretty girls with pastel mouths and rouged cheeks wearing waistless petal-hemmed dresses, their hair marcelled in finger-waves, and as they flit from party to party they step in and out of obedient taxis driven by men only too happy to accept a penny tip. It was unlikely those women ever came as far north as West Hampstead or Kilburn, and I think Hampstead wasn't fashionable then, though in D. H. Lawrence's stories artists and writers live there. What is astonishing about reminiscences of those times is not only that there were different Londons for the poor and the middle class, let alone the rich, but the pedlars of memories never seem to be aware of this: 'In those days, when I was a little girl, I used to scrub steps. I did even when it was snowing, and I had bare feet, they were blue with cold sometimes, and I went to the baker's for yesterday's bread, cheap, and my poor little mother slaved sixteen hours a day, six days a week, oh those were wicked times, cruel times they were.' 'In those days we were proud to live in London. Now it's just horrid, full of horrid people.'

In my half of the carriage are three white people and
the rest are black and brown and yellowish. Or, by another
division, five females and six males. Or, four young people
and seven middle-aged or elderly. Two Japanese girls, as
glossy and self-sufficient as young cats, sit smiling. Surely
the mourners for old London must applaud the Japanese,
who are never, ever, scruffy or careless? Probably not: in
that other London there were no foreigners, only English,
pinko-grey as Shaw said, always *chez nous*, for the Empire
had not imploded, the world had not invaded, and while
every family had at least one relative abroad administering
colonies or dominions, or being soldiers, that was abroad,
it was there, not here, the colonies had not come home
to roost.

These Japanese girls are inside an invisible bubble, they
look out from a safe world. When I was in Japan I met many
Japanese young ladies, who all seemed concerned to be
Yum Yum. They giggled and went oooh – oooh – oooh
as they jumped up and down, goody goody, and gently
squealed with pleasure or with shock. But if you got them
by themselves they were tough young women with a sharp
view of life. Not that it was easy, for there always hovered
some professor or mentor concerned to return them to
their group, keep them safe and corporate.

A young black man sits dreaming, his ears wired to
his Walkman, and his feet jig gently to some private
rhythm. He wears clothes more expensive, more stylish,
than anyone else in this travelling room. Next to him is
an Indian woman with a girl of ten or so. They wear
saris that show brown midriffs as glossy as toffee, but
they have cardigans over them. Butterfly saris, workaday
cardigans that make the statement, if you choose to live
in a cold northern country, then this is the penalty. Never
has there been a sadder sartorial marriage than saris with
cardigans. They sit quietly conversing, in a way that makes

the little girl seem a woman. These three get out at Finchley Road. In get four Americans, two boys, two girls, in their uniform of jeans and T-shirts and sports shoes. They talk loudly and do not see anyone else. Two sprawl opposite, and two loll on either side of, a tall old woman, possibly Scottish, who sits with her burnished shoes side by side, her fine bony hands on the handle of a wheeled shopping basket. She gazes ahead of her, as if the loud youngsters do not exist, and she is possibly remembering – but what London? The war? (Second World War, this time.) Not a poor London, that is certain. She is elegant, in tweeds and a silk shirt and her rings are fine. She and the four Americans get out at St John's Wood, the youngsters off to the American School, but she probably lives here. St John's Wood, so we are told by Galsworthy, for one, was where kept women were put in discreetly pretty villas by rich or at least respectable lovers. Now these villas can be afforded only by the rich, often Arabs.

As people get into the waiting train, I sit remembering how not long ago I visited a French friend in a St John's Wood hotel. While I stood at the reception desk three Arabs in white robes went through from a back part of the hotel to the lift, carrying at shoulder level a tray heaped with rice, and on that a whole roasted sheep. The lobby swooned with the smell of spices and roast meat. The receptionist said, to my enquiring look, 'Oh, it's for Sheikh So-and-So, he has a feast every night.' And she continued to chat on the telephone to a boyfriend. 'Oh, you only say that, oh I know all about men, you can't tell me anything' – using these words, as far as she was concerned, for the first time in history. And she caressed the hair above her left ear with a complacent white hand that had on it a lump of synthetic amber the size of a hen's egg. Her shining hair was amber, cut in a 1920s shingle. Four more Arabs flowed past, their long brown fingers playing with their prayer beads, like nuns who repel the world with their rosaries. 'Hail Mary Full of Grace ...' their lips moving as they smile and nod, talking part in worldly conversation: but their fingers holding tight to righteousness. The Arabs disappeared into the lift, presumably on their way to the feast, while the revolving doors admitted four more, a congregation of sheikhs.

Not far from here, in Abbey Road, are the studios where the Beatles recorded. At the pedestrian crossing made famous by the Four are always platoons of tourists, of all ages and races, standing to stare with their souls in their eyes, while their fingers go click-click on their cameras. All over the world, in thousands of albums, are cherished photographs of this dingy place.

This part of London is not old. When the villas were full of mistresses and ladies of pleasure it was a newish suburb. Travelling from NW6 or NW2 into the centre is to leave recently settled suburbs for the London that has risen and fallen in successive incarnations since before the Romans. Not long ago I was at lunch in the house that was Gladstone's, now a Press Club. For most of us it is hard to imagine a family actually living in a house that seems built only to present people for public occasions, but above all, no one could stand on Carlton House Terrace and think: Not long ago there was a wood here, running water, grazing beasts. No, Nature is away down a flight of grandiose steps, across the Mall, and kept well in its place in St James's Park. The weight of those buildings, pavements, roads, forbids thoughts of the kind still so natural in St John's Wood, where you think: there must have been a wood here, and who was St John? – almost certainly a church. Easy to see the many trees as survivors of that wood: unlikely, but not impossible.

Today I am glad I am not getting off here. The escalator

often doesn't work. Only a month ago, on one of the blackboards the staff use to communicate their thoughts to passengers was written in jaunty white chalk: 'You are probably wondering why the escalators so often aren't working? We shall tell you! It is because they are old and often go out of order. Sorry! Have a good day!' Which message, absolutely in the style of London humour, sardonic and with its edge of brutality, was enough to cheer one up, and ready to make the long descent on foot.

In jump three youngsters. Yobbos. Louts. Hooligans. They are sixteen or so, in other words adolescents, male, with their loud raucous unhappy braying laughter, their raging sex, their savagery. Two white and a black. Their cries, their jeers, command everyone's attention – which is after all the point. One white youth and the black are jostling and the third, who puts up with it in a manner of stylized resignation, smiling like a sophisticated Christian martyr: probably some film or television hero. Impossible to understand what they are saying, for their speech is as unformed as if they had speech defects – probably intentionally, for who wants to be understood too well by adults at sixteen? All this aggro is only horseplay, on the edge of harm, no more. At Baker Street the two tormentors push out the third, try to prevent him from re-entering. Not so easy, this, for trains take their time at Baker Street, the all-purpose junction for many-suburbed London. The three tire of the scuffle and step inside to stand near the door, preventing others from entering, but only by their passivity. Excuse me, excuse me, travellers say, confronted by these three large youths who neither resist nor attack, but only take up a lot of room, knowing that they do, knowing they are a damned nuisance, but preserving innocent faces that ignore mutters and angry stares. As the doors begin to close, the two aggressors push out the victim, and stand making all kinds of abusive gestures at him, and mouthing silent insults as the train starts to move. The lad on the platform shouts insults back but points in the direction the train is going, presumably to some agreed destination. As we gather speed he is half-strolling, half-dancing, along the platform, and he sends a forked-fingered gesture after us. The two seem to miss him, and they sit loosely, gathering energy for the next explosion, which occurs at Bond Street, where they are off the train in dangerous kangaroo leaps, shouting abuse. At whom? Does it matter? Where they sat roll two soft-drink cans, as bright and seductive as advertisements. Now in the coach are people who have not seen the whole sequence, and they are probably thinking, Thank God I shall never have to be that age again! Or are they? Is it possible that when people sigh, Oh if only I was young again, they are regretting what we have just seen, but remembered as an interior landscape of limitless possibilities?

At Bond Street a lot of people get out, and the train stays still long enough to read comfortably the poem provided by the Keepers of the Underground, inserted into a row of advertisements.

THE EAGLE

He clasps the crag with crooked hands:
Close to the sun in lonely lands.
Ring'd with the azure world he stands.

The wrinkled sea beneath him crawls:
He watches from his mountain walls.
And like a thunderbolt he falls.

Alfred Lord Tennyson

In get a crowd of Danish school-children, perhaps on a day trip. They are well-behaved, and watched over by a smiling girl, who does not seem much older than they are. Tidily they descend at Green Park, and the carriage fills up again. All tourists. Is that what people mean when they complain the Underground is so untidy? It is the xenophobia of the British again? Rather, the older generations of the British. Is what I enjoy about London, its variety, its populations from everywhere in the world, its transitoriness – for sometimes London can give you the same feeling as when you stand to watch cloud shadows chase across a plain – exactly what they so hate?

Yet for people so threatened they are doing, I think, rather well. Not long ago I saw this incident. It was a large London hospital, in a geriatric ward. 'I'm just on my way to Geriatrics' you may hear one sprightly young nurse tell another, as she darts her finger to the lift button. An old white woman, brought in because she had fallen, was being offered a bedpan. She was not only old, in fact ancient, and therefore by rights an inhabitant of that lost Eden of decently uniform pinko-grey people, but working class and a spinster. (One may still see women described on old documents, Status: Spinster.) For such a woman to be invited to use a bedpan in a public place before the curtains had even been drawn about her was bad enough. To be nursed by a man, a male nurse, something she had never imagined possible. Worst of all, he was black, a young calm black man, in a nurse's uniform. ('No, I'm not a doctor, I'm a nurse – yes, that's right, a nurse.') He turned back the bed covers, assisted the old woman on to the bedpan, nicely pulling down her nightgown over her old thighs, and drew the curtains. 'I'll be back in just a minute, love.' And off he went. Behind that curtain went on an internal drama hard to imagine by people used to polyglot and casually mannered London, whether they enjoy it or not. When he returned to pull back the curtains, ask if she was all right – did she want him to clean her up a little? – and then remove the pan, her eyes were bright with dignified defiance. She had come to terms with the impossible. 'No, dear, it's all right, I can still do that for myself.'

In a school in South London where a friend is governor, twenty-five languages are spoken.

Now we are tunnelling under old London, though not the oldest, for that is a mile, or two or three, further East. On the other side of thick shelves of earth as full of pipes and cables, wires, sewers, the detritus of former buildings and towns as garden soil is of worms and roots, is St James's Park – Downing Street – Whitehall. If someone travelled these under-earth galleries and never came up into the air it would be easy to believe this was all there could be to life, to living. There is a sci-fi story about a planet where suns and moons appear only every so many years, and the citizens wait for the miracle, the revelation of their situation in the universe, which of course the priests have taken possession of, claiming the splendour of stars as proof of their right to rule. There are already cities where an under-earth town repeats the one above it, built in air – for instance, Houston, Texas. You enter an unremarkable door, just as in a dream, and you are in an underground city, miles of it, with shops, restaurants, offices. You need never come up. There are people who actually like basement flats, choose them, draw curtains, turn on lights, create for themselves an underground, and to them above-ground living seems as dangerous as ordinary life does to an ex-prisoner or someone too long in hospital. They institutionalize themselves, create a place where everything is controlled by them, a calm concealed place, away from critical eyes, and the hazards of weather and the changes of light are shut out. Unless the machinery fails: a gas leak, the telephone goes wrong.

In the fifties I knew a man who spent all day going

around the Circle Line. It was like a job, a discipline, from nine till six. *They* couldn't get at him, he claimed. He was having a breakdown. Did people go in for more imaginative breakdowns, then? It sometimes seems a certain flair has gone out of the business. And yet, a few days ago, on the Heath, there approached a Saxon – well, a young man wearing clothes it would be possible to agree Saxons might have worn. A brown woollen shirt. Over it a belted jerkin contrived from thick brown paper. Breeches were made with elastic bands up the calves. A draped brown scarf made a monkish hood. He held a spear from a toy shop. 'Prithee, kind sir,' said my companion, somewhat out of period, 'whither goest thou?' The young Saxon stopped, delighted and smiling, while his companion, a young woman full of concern, looked on. 'Out,' said the young man. 'Away.'

'What is your name? Beowulf? Olaf the Red? Eric the Brave?'

'Eric the Black.'

'It isn't your name *really*,' said his minder, claiming him for fact.

'Yes it is,' we heard as they wandered off into the russets, the yellows, the scorched greens of the unforgettable autumn of 1990. 'My name is Eric, isn't it? Well then, it *is* Eric.'

Charing Cross and everyone gets out. At the exit machine a girl appears running up from the deeper levels, and she is chirping like an alarm. Now she has drawn our attention to it, in fact a steady bleeping is going on, and for all we know, it is a fire alarm. These days there are so many electronic bleeps, cheeps, buzzes, blurps, that we don't hear them. The girl is a fey creature, blonde locks flying around a flushed face. She is laughing dizzily, and racing a flight or flock of young things coming into the West End for an evening's adventure, all of them already

crazed with pleasure, and in another dimension of speed
and lightness, like sparks speeding up and out. She and
two girls push in their tickets and flee along a tunnel to
the upper world, but three youths vault over, with cries of
triumph, and their state of being young is such a claim on
us all that the attendant decides not to notice, for it would
be as mad as swatting butterflies.

Now I am going out to Trafalgar Square, along a tunnel,
and there, against a wall, is a site where groups of youngsters are always bending, crouching, squatting, to examine
goods laid on boxes, and bits of cloth. Rings and earrings,
bracelets, brooches, all kinds of glitter and glitz, brass and
glass, white metal and cheap silver, cheap things but full
of promise and possibility.

I follow this tunnel and that, go up some steps, and I
am in Trafalgar Square. Ahead of me across the great grey
space with its low pale fountains is the National Gallery,
and near it the National Portrait Gallery. The sky is a light
blue, sparkling, and fragile clouds are being blown about
by winds at work far above our level of living, for down
here it is quiet. Now I may enjoyably let time slide away
in one Gallery or both, and not decide till the last possible
moment, shall I turn left to the National, or walk another
fifty paces and look at the faces of our history? When I
come out, the sky, though it will not have lost light, will
have acquired an intense late-afternoon look, time to find
a café, to meet friends and then . . . in an hour or so the
curtain will go up in a theatre, or the English National
Opera. Still, after all these years, these decades, there is
no moment like that when the curtain goes up, the house
lights dim . . . Or, having dawdled about, one can after all
simply go home, taking care to miss the rush hour.

Not long ago, at the height of the rush hour, I was
strap-hanging, and in that half of the carriage, that is,
among fourteen people, three people read books among

all the newspapers. In the morning, off to work, people betray their allegiances: *The Times*, the *Independent*, the *Guardian*, the *Telegraph*, the *Mail*. The bad papers some of us are ashamed of don't seem much in evidence, but then this is a classy line, at least at some hours and in some stretches of it. At night the *Evening Standard* adds itself to the display. Three people. At my right elbow a man was reading the *Iliad*. Across the aisle a woman read *Moby Dick*. As I pushed out, a girl held up *Wuthering Heights* over the head of a new baby asleep on her chest. When people talk glumly about our state of illiteracy I tell them I saw this, and they are pleased, but sceptical.

The poem holding its own among the advertisements was:

INFANT JOY

'I have no name:
I am but two days old.'
What shall I call thee?
'I happy am.
Joy is my name.'
Sweet joy befall thee!

Pretty joy!
Sweet joy but two days old.
Sweet joy I call thee:
Thou dost smile.
I sing the while
Sweet joy befall thee.

William Blake

Walking back from the Underground I pass three churches. Two of them are no longer conduits for celestial currents:

one is a theatre, one derelict. In such a small bit of
London, three churches ... that other-worldly visitor so
useful for enlivening our organs of comparison might,
seventy years ago, have wondered, 'What are they for,
these buildings, so like each other, so unlike all the others,
several to a district? Administrative buildings? A network
of governmental offices? Newly built, too!' But these days
this person, she, he or it, would note the buildings are
often unused. 'A change of government perhaps?' Yet
certain types of buildings repeat themselves from one
end of the city to the other. 'Just as I saw on my last visit,
there are "pubs" for dispensing intoxicants, and centres
for fast movement by means of rail. Others are for the
maintenance of machines like metal bugs or beetles – a
new thing this, nothing like that last time I was here. And
there is another new thing. Every few yards is a centre for
the sale of drugs, chemical substances.' A funny business
– he, she or it might muse, mentally arranging the items
of the report that will be faxed back to Canopus. 'If I put
them in order of frequency of occurrence, then chemists'
shops must come first. This is a species dependent on
chemical additions to what they eat and drink.' Within
a mile of where I live there are at least fifteen chemists'
shops, and every grocery has shelves of medicines.

As I turn the corner past where the old mill stood I leave
behind the stink and roar of vehicles pushing their way
northwards and I realize that for some minutes it has
been unpleasant to breathe. Now Mill Lane, where shops
are always starting up, going bankrupt, changing hands,
particularly now with the trebling and quadrupling of
rents and rates. Soon, I am in the little roads full of houses,
and the traffic has become a steady but minor din. The
streets here are classically inclined. Agamemnon, Achilles,
Ulysses, and there is an Orestes Mews. Add to these names
Gondar, and one may postulate an army man, classically

educated, who was given the job of naming these streets. In fact, this was not so far wrong. The story was this. (True or false? Who cares? Every story of the past, recent or old, is bound to be tidied up, rounded off, made consequential.) An ex-army man, minor gentry, had a wife in the country with many children, and a mistress in town, with many more. To educate all these he went in for property, bought farmland that spread attractively over a hill with views of London, and built what must have been one of the first northern commuter suburbs . . . for remember, in the valley just down from this hill, towards London, were the streams, the cows and the green fields my old friend took a penny bus ride to visit every Sunday. The commuters went in by horse-bus or by train to the City.

Some of the buildings are Mansions, built from the start as flats, but most were houses, since converted into three flats. Hard to work out how these houses functioned. The cellars are all wet. In mine labels come off bottles in three months. Yet there was a lavatory down here. Used by whom? Surely nobody could have lived in this earthy cave? Perhaps it wasn't wet then. Now a circular hole or mini shaft has been dug into the soil, for the damp has long ago heaved off the cement floor, and in it one may watch the water level rise and fall. Not according to the rainfall: all of us in this area know the tides have something to do with the leaking pipes of the reservoir, which from my top window looks like an enormous green field, or village green, for there are great trees all around it: the Victorians put their reservoirs underground. (They say that if you know the man who has the task of guarding the precious waters, one may be taken through a small door and find oneself on the edge of a reach of still black water, under a low ceiling where lights gleam down. One may add to this attractively theatrical picture the faint plop of a rat swimming away from sudden light, and a single slow-spreading ripple.) The top of my house is a converted attic. But the attics were not converted then. There are three bedrooms on the second floor, one too small to share. Two rooms on the first floor, now one room, but then probably dining room and sitting room. A kitchen is pleasantly but inconveniently off a veranda or 'patio' – a recent addition. It was not a kitchen then. On the ground floor is one room, once two, and 'conveniences' also added recently. A garden room, most likely a nursery. In those days they had so many children, they often had relatives living with them, and every middle-class household had at least one servant, usually more. How were they all fitted in? Where did they cook, where was the larder, how did they get the washing done? And how did they keep warm? There are minuscule fire baskets in small fireplaces in every room.

A hundred years ago this suburb, these houses, were built, and they are solid and thick-walled and all the builders who come to mend roofs or fix plumbing tell you how well they were put up, how good the materials were. 'We don't build like that now.' Nor are these experts dismayed by the wet cellar. 'You keep that clay good and wet around your foundations, and it won't shrink in these summers we are having now, and you won't be sorry.'

As I turn the corner into the street I live in the light is arranging the clouds into tinted masses. The sunsets up here are, to say the least, satisfactory.

Ivy loads the corner house, and starlings are crowding themselves in there, swooping out, swirling back, to become invisible and silent until the morning.

T*he New Café*

There is a new café in our main street, Stephanie's, a year old now, and always full. It is French, like the 'Boucherie' next to it – a very British butcher – like the 'Brasserie' opposite, and it is run by two Greeks. At once it acquired its regulars, of whom I am one. Here, as in all good cafés, may be observed real-life soap operas, to be defined as series of emotional events that are certainly not unfamiliar, since you are bound to have seen something like them before, but to which you lack the key that will make them not trite, but shockingly individual.

The miraculous summer of 1989, when one hot blue day followed another, made pavement life as intense as in Paris or Rome, and our café had tables outside crammed against the aromatic offerings of a greengrocer. There everyone prefers to sit, but you are lucky to find a seat. Early in the summer two German girls appeared, large, attractive, uninhibitedly in search of boyfriends for their holidays. They were always together, usually outside, and for a few days sat alone eating the delicious cakes – genuinely French – that none can resist. They were delighted when someone – anyone – said, 'Is this chair free?' Once this was me. They had three weeks in London.

They were in a small hotel ten minutes away. They thought London was a fine place. The weather was wonderful and – look! – how brown we are getting. While we chatted their eyes at once flew to anyone coming in.

And then they were with a young man. I had seen him here before. He sometimes dropped in for a coffee and was off at once. The German girls liked him. They leaned forward on their large and confident behinds and laughed and flung back blonde manes and all their rows of dewy teeth shone out at everybody. For they continued to keep an eye on possibilities. He leaned back in his chair, and entertained them. 'I like that one,' you could imagine one girl saying to another. 'He is a joker, I think?'

He was a likeable man, perhaps twenty-seven or eight, blue-eyed, fair haired – all that kind of thing, but he had about him something that said, Keep Off. He was a little like a young hawk that hasn't yet got the hang of it, with a fluffy apprentice fierceness. And he was restless, always hooking and unhooking his legs, or flinging them hastily to one side to get them out of the way of someone coming past, or who seemed to sit too close.

For a few days the three of them were together, usually in the early afternoon. When they left, a girl was on either side of him. But there ought to be a fourth, and soon there he was. When the four met, inside the café or on the pavement, it did not seem as if they had paired off. The girls still kept their eyes on the entertainer, their bright mouths smiling in anticipation for the moment they could laugh, for that is what they liked best to do. And he sat watching them laugh, pleased he was giving them what they wanted, and the other young man, who did not seem to hope for much, laughed too.

Once or twice they ate a proper meal. Sometimes they talked about a film they had seen. One afternoon he came in with a dark composed girl who had a sisterly and satiric air. He bought her coffee and cakes and seemed apologetic about something. When the German girls came in he waved at them, tucked away his legs like an awkward parcel to make room, and the three girls and the man stayed for a time, and then went off together. Thereafter I saw him with the dark girl and with other girls and he treated them as he did the German girls, for he seemed to like them all.

Once two tables outside were empty and I sat at one and soon he was at the other, dropping into a chair at the last moment as he went past, as if he might as well do that as anything else. By now we were café acquaintances. He remarked that the summer wasn't bad at all and he was glad he hadn't gone to Spain, for it was better here. There was a week left of his holiday. He worked at the builders' supply shop down the road. It wasn't bad, he quite liked it. Sitting close to him in the strong light it could be seen that he was older than he seemed. There were lines under his eyes, and he was often abstracted, as if he were continually being removed from present surroundings by an inner buzzer: attend to this.

The German girls arrived and they were laughing in anticipation before they sat down.

Then they were not coming to the café, and he was back at work. He dropped in once or twice with a colleague from work, two young men wearing very white boiler suits, which were to make them look knowledgeable about building materials. The German girls' young man seemed frail inside the thick suit.

One day I was standing outside the Underground station, waiting to meet someone. He strolled past, taking his time, preoccupied. Then his face spread in a smile so unlike anything I had seen there, I quickly turned. Just ahead of him on the pavement was a young girl with a pram. No, when you looked she was a small pale young woman, probably twenty, and she was the baby's mother, from the tender way she bent to tuck it into already overwhelming covers. She smiled at the concealed baby, and then turned, startled, as the man came up and said in his whimsical, don't-take-me-seriously way, 'Hilda, it's me.' The two stood, dissolved in smiles. In a moment they would be in an embrace, but she recovered herself and quickly stood back. Then he, too, put on responsibility, as if fitting a winter's coat over his white boiler suit. Because he could not, apparently, embrace the mother, he leaned over the pram with a gallant air, and she leaned past him, lifted a bundle from its depths, and held the baby so that he could see its face. He bent politely over it and made appropriate noises, laughing at himself so that she had to laugh too. But all the time his eyes were on the young mother. She laughed again and pretended to thrust the baby at him for him to hold. At which he staggered back in a pantomime of an embarrassed male, and she fussed the bundle back under its covers and stood soberly, confronting him. He too was serious. They stood there a long time, long at least for an observer, perhaps a minute or more, looking at each other, entranced. These two were a match, a fit, the same kind: you had to say about them as you do, rarely, say about a couple: they are two halves of a whole, they belong together.

Again it was she who recovered herself and pushed the pram away down the pavement. Slowly pushed. After a few steps she turned to look at him. On she went – but turned again. He still stood there, gazing after her. She gave him a brave little wave, and went on. Slower, slower . . . but she had to go on, she had to, and she reached the corner much too soon, where she stopped and looked back to where he stood, his face as miserable as hers. Again the seconds sped past . . . But at last she firmly pushed the pram on and away and disappeared. Never has there been a corner of a street as empty as that one. He stared. She had gone. He took two steps to go after her, then came back, sending over his shoulder a quick glance: yes, she really had gone.

Slowly he walked on, slower, and stopped. He was level with me. He wasn't seeing anybody or anything, he was inside himself. He stood with his knees slightly bent, his arms loose, palms showing, his head back, as if he planned at some point to raise his eyes to the sky.

On the face of the charmed man chased emotions. There was regret, but a self-consciously dandyish regret, for even in his extremity he was not going to let go of this lifeline. There was bewilderment. There was loss. Above all, tenderness, banishing the others. Meanwhile his forehead was tense and his eyes sombre. What was he thinking? 'What was all that? What? But what happened ... what *did* happen, I don't understand what happened ... I don't understand ...'

Something like that.

Romance 1988

Two young women sat on opposite sides of a table in the cafeteria in Terminal Three, Heathrow airport. They were in the raised part, which is like a little stage. Sybil had gone straight to this area though there were places empty in the lower, less emphasized, part of the room.

They were sisters, both large-boned, stocky, with broad sensible faces. But Sybil refused to be ordinary, wore dramatic makeup, short yellow hair, clothes you had to look at. She was a dazzler, like a pop star. No one would particularly notice Joan, and she sat admiring Sybil and giving London full credit, at least for this: they were from northern England, and they valued this sound inheritance, so much better than anything the frivolous and spoiled south could produce. They were in the old tradition of two sisters, the pretty one and the clever one, and so they had been cast in their childhoods – Joan, clever, and Sybil, pretty. But they were both clever attractive hard-working girls who pursued their chances with skill.

Joan was saying, 'But you're only twenty-two. I thought you were going to take your time?' She was the older sister, twenty-four.

Sybil said in her loud careless voice that everyone had

to listen to, always, 'But my dear, I'll never find anyone like Oliver, I know that.'

Joan smiled. Deliberately. She raised her brows.

Sybil grinned at her, acknowledging the older sister act.

They did not need to hurry this conversation. Joan was on her way to Bahrain where she had got herself a job as secretary in a part-American, part-English firm. She had just flown in from Yorkshire, and there were three hours before her flight out. Sybil had said that of course she would come out to Heathrow to be with her sister, no, it didn't matter, she just wouldn't go to work that day. She had arrived in London two years before and had at once taken possession of it, getting herself – God only knew how – a secondhand car, and she thought nothing of driving out to the airport at six in the morning or eleven at night to have a chat with friends who were always on their way through, or of dropping in on several parties in one night, in places as far apart as Greenwich and Chiswick. She had come to London as a secretary, but had decided that 'temping' was a better bet. Thus one sampled all kinds of different work, met a lot of different men, and when she was offered a job that suited her she would stay put. At least, that was what she had said until recently.

'You said all that about Geoff, remember,' said Joan, not unpleasantly, but putting the case.

'Oh *God*,' said Sybil, 'but I was only an infant then.'

'Eighteen,' said Joan.

'All right! Granted! And I know it doesn't sound likely, but we are made for each other, Oliver and I.'

'Has he said so?'

'I think we're in for it – marriage, kids, a mortgage, the lot.' The loud confident voice was attracting attention, and Joan was embarrassed. As she had been, all her life, by her sister.

She said in a pointedly low voice, 'Sybil, you told me it was all off with Oliver.'

'Yes, I know I did,' said Sybil loudly. 'He said he didn't want to marry again. He liked being free. And off he went. I didn't see him for months. He broke my heart. When he came after me again I said to him, You've broken my heart once, so this time you're going to have to make the running, I'm not coming after you. Not the way I did when I first met him,' she explained. And she cast a glance around to make sure her audience was still rapt.

Joan considered all this. Then she asked, 'When you're married, are you going to travel abroad with him when he's on his trips?'

Oliver travelled a great deal for his firm, was more often away than in London.

'No. Oh well, I'll go with him sometimes, if it's somewhere interesting, but I'll make a home for him in London. No, I'm going to be a real wife,' she insisted, to her sister's quizzical smile.

'You always have to go to extremes.'

'What's extreme about that?'

'If you can't see it's over the top! Anyway, last time you said whenever he went abroad he took a different girl.'

'Yes, I know. He was in Rome last week and I knew he had slept with someone though he didn't say and I didn't ask. Because it was not my business . . .' Joan was looking so humorous that it was with an effect of shouting against noise that Sybil went on, '*Yes*. But then he confessed he had slept with someone and he felt guilty about it. Because of me. And I've been feeling guilty if I slept with anyone but him right from the very first time I slept with him.'

'Well,' sighed Joan, 'I suppose that's pretty conclusive.'

'Yes, I think it is. And what about you and Derek? Is he going to wait until you get back from Bahrain?'

'He says he will, but I have my doubts.'

They smiled at each other.

'Plenty of fish in the sea,' said Sybil.

'He's all right. But I reckon I'll have saved up thirty thousand out there, that is if I stick it out. There's nothing to spend anything on.'

'And then you'll be independent.'

'Yes. I'll buy a house the moment I get back.'

'Makes sense. And Oliver and I are looking for a house. We were looking last Sunday. It's fun looking at houses. There was one I think he would settle for, but I said to him, No, if we are going to be Upwardly Mobile, then let's *do* it. That house isn't good enough. You're doing better and better all the time, I said to him. Because he is. He's shooting up in his firm, and he gets more and more eligible every day.'

'You always did say you would marry for money.'

'Yes, I did. And I am. But I wouldn't marry him if I didn't feel like this about him.'

'But do you feel like this about him because he is so eligible?' enquired Joan, laughing.

'Probably. But what's the matter with that?'

'Would you marry him if he was poor?'

The sisters were now leaning forward, faces close, laughing and full of enjoyment.

'No, I wouldn't. I've got to have money. I know myself, don't I?'

'I hope you do,' said the older sister, suddenly sober.

Meanwhile people nearby were smiling at each other because of the two young adventurers, probably feeling that they ought to be shocked or something.

There was a pause, while they attended to coffee, croissants, fruit juice.

And then, suddenly, Sybil announced, 'And we are both going to have an AIDS test.' Now the people listening stopped smiling, though they were certainly attending.

'We both decided, at the same time. I mentioned it first, and found he had thought of it too. He slept around a lot after his divorce, and I have too, since I came to London. And you never know. But the trouble is, I'm going to have it done privately, because if it's on the National Health then it's in the records for everyone to see. Because then it would look as if you were worried.'

'And it's expensive.'

'Yes. Well, I can't afford it, I don't have the money, but Oliver can and he'll pay for me.'

Joan smiled. 'Certainly one way of making him responsible for you.'

'Yes, it is.'

'What will you do if either of you is positive?'

'Oh, I'm sure we won't be! We're both as hetero as they come. But you never know. We want to be on the safe side. No, we'll have the tests done and then we'll give each other our certificates.' Her face was soft and dreamy, full of love. For the first time she had forgotten her audience.

'Well,' said Joan, taking neat little sips of coffee, 'I suppose that's one way of doing it.'

'It means much more than an engagement ring, I mean, it's a real commitment.'

'And he is going to have to be faithful to you now, isn't he?'

'But I'll have to be faithful to him!'

Joan's face was suggesting this was not the same thing. Then she asked, teasing, 'Faithful for ever?'

'Yes . . . well . . . for as long as we can, anyway. We don't want to sleep with anyone else, not the way we feel now. What's the point of risking it, anyway?'

She glanced around, but her audience no longer attended to her. They were talking to each other. If this was their way of showing disapproval, then . . .

Two and a half hours to go.

Sybil raised her voice. 'We tried condoms, too, but God knows how people get them to work. We laughed so much that in the end we simply had to settle for going to sleep.'

'Shhhhh,' said Joan, in agony. 'Shhhhhh.'

'Why? What's the matter, no, let me tell you, if the safety of the nation is going to depend on condoms, then . . .'

At this point a young man who had been sitting near them, listening, got up because it was time for him to be off on his way to somewhere or other in the world. He tapped Sybil on the shoulder and said, 'If you can't get the hang of condoms, then just get in touch with me . . . no, no, any time, a pleasure!'

His words were far from an invitation, were more of a public rebuke, and on his face was the look that goes with someone taking it on himself to keep things in order. But from the door he sent them a glance and a grin and disappeared for ever with a wave. As for Joan and Sybil, they sat half turned to watch him go. They looked like a couple of teenagers, their hands half-covering scandalized and delighted smiles.

What Price the Truth?

I want to tell you something, I have to tell *someone*. *I have to talk.* I suddenly understood you are the only person left who will know what I'm talking about. Has that happened to you? You suddenly think, My God, that was twenty, thirty years ago and I am the only person left who knows what really happened?

Do you remember Caesar? Remember I worked for him? Do you – most people have forgotten. We called him Caesar . . . he never knew it of course. Because he used to say, I'm going to conquer Britain – remember that? If you do, then you and I are the only people left who do. Well, Caesar's son married my daughter last weekend . . . yes, exactly, you can't improve on life, can you, Life: God's little script-writer. But you only know the half of it, *listen*.

Did you ever meet Robert, Caesar's son? If you did, he must have been an infant. Well, he's turned out a charming boy, sweet, but really, really nice.

Ten years ago he rang me at the office and asked me out to dinner. He was fourteen. I was struck dumb. Well, as far as I can be struck dumb. I was so *tickled* – of course I said yes. But wait until you hear where. It was at the

Berengaria. Yes, quite so. I don't know what I expected, but he did it all perfectly. He might have been thirty-five, this kid, this *baby*, he called for me in a taxi with flowers, in a hired suit. He had booked a table and gone in to discuss it all with the head waiter. The waiters were hovering about like nannies, they were tickled out of their wits, because of this kid and me – of course they knew me for years, I used to go there with Caesar, or I went in to arrange special dinners for him. He used to talk as if it was *his* restaurant . . . are you getting the picture? Not by a nod or a beck did the waiters embarrass him, they were wonderful. I sat there going mad with curiosity. *Fourteen*. Then I thought, All right, we are all mad at fourteen, forget it. And I was busy then, as usual. But it must have cost him fifty quid. Where did he get it? Not from his father, that mean old . . .

The next thing, he writes me a letter on best quality ivory vellum notepaper, with his name printed on it, Robert Meredith Stone, asking me to go for a walk in St James's Park, and then tea at the Ritz. Wait a minute, I thought, just wait a minute . . . it's time to do some thinking.

Dinner at the Berengaria fair enough, it was Caesar's place, but a walk in the *park*? Caesar has never set foot off a London pavement. He probably doesn't know a daffodil from a rose. In his old age he sits like a sour old goat grumping at 1930s films on the video, don't imagine he limps about the garden philosophizing while he prunes the roses. Marie has always done the gardening.

I thought it all over, but really *thought*, and then I asked Marie for lunch. I needed to talk to her without Caesar knowing, I didn't want to give poor Robert away.

I hadn't seen Marie for years. We always got on, if you can call it that, having nothing in common but behaving well. She's old these days, she's decided to be an old woman. I'm damned if I will yet. I mean, it's a lot of effort to let yourself get old, you have to change your clothes, your style, everything, it's all right for her, she's got time for all that, she's never had to work in her life. Of course she was curious to know what it was all about and I didn't know how to start. As soon as I saw her I realized I couldn't ask. What was I to say? Tell me, does your Robert think that your Caesar and I had an affair and if so, what's all this about strolls in St James's Park and feeding the ducks?

She thought it was ever so sweet of me to ask her for lunch, but she's got vague, she started to talk about Caesar's girlfriends. 'I never minded,' said she, 'not after the first . . .' And then she made a joke, yes, actually a joke, 'It's the first one that counts, you know, *le premier pas qui coûte*, and he always had such nice women,' paying me a compliment, *noblesse oblige*. 'And I never did like sex,' she says, 'or perhaps I wasn't lucky with Caesar, or he wasn't lucky with me.' I swear she was ready for me to tell her how I had found her Caesar in bed, and I understood something at that moment, it struck me all of a heap, it struck me dumb – yes, all right, but I told you I had to *talk*. Now, this is the point. It was always important to me that I never slept with Caesar, but it was exactly at that moment, eating a healthful salad with Caesar's wife . . . ha ha, how absolutely apropos . . . that I knew how important it was, a point of pride. And now it mattered to her so little she didn't even remember I had gone to her and said, Look here, Marie, I don't know what anyone else thinks and I don't care, but it matters to me what *you* think: I am not sleeping with your husband, and I never did. She didn't remember I had gone specially to tell her. She looked at me vaguely, and said, 'Oh yes? Did you? Funny, I forget things . . . but I didn't mind, you know.' She minded all right. She's decided to forget that. Whether she believed me or not she minded like hell and I minded her minding. Because I was innocent. It was just the same having lunch with her as it was *then* – because the one thing I couldn't say was, the most important, your husband is a mean, scrimping, pennywise tightfist, and he's killed me with overwork, he always has to work people he employs to the bone, and he has to underpay them. Never mind about sleeping with me, I would have liked to say, then and at lunch that day, but working with that little Scrooge never left much energy for sex.

Have you forgotten how it was with me then? I had two kids – but *do* you remember? The funny thing is, meeting people in public life, professional life, you meet them as individuals, but what's important about them, often, is what you don't see. In my case it was two small children and an ex-husband who sometimes came through with a few quid but more often didn't. I was being paid a senior typist's wage when I ran Caesar's office for him. I was his Girl Friday, I organized everything, and it was I who had the contacts, I knew everyone in the field when he was a newcomer in it. I used to set up whole shows for him, and he'd take the credit. I used to work from eight in the morning till eleven, twelve, one at night. I made that man and he knew it too, but if he'd paid me, he'd be admitting just what my real worth to him was. I'm not saying he wouldn't have succeeded without me, but if he conquered Britain – because he did, *we* did, he was known everywhere and not just in this country, he was a name in France and Germany – if he did all that it was because of me. Then one day I was so exhausted I couldn't get out of bed. I telephoned the office and said right, that was it, I was giving him notice, I couldn't stand it. I had to get a job that paid me properly. I was in debt for the rent. I couldn't even pay for the children's clothes, and their father had been out of work for months – he was an actor, it wasn't his fault. Suddenly there is Caesar ringing the doorbell, for the first time, and I'd been working for him ten years then. He comes in, he looks around. Two rooms and a bathroom, oh yes, it was a decent little place, I wasn't going to let the kids go without, but I slept in the living room and they had the other room. 'Nice place,' says Caesar, sniffing about pricing everything, 'you do yourself well.' And he with his bloody great house at Richmond. I got back into bed and actually went to sleep, I was so *ill* I didn't care. 'You can't just give me notice,' he says, waking me up. 'I am giving you notice,' I say. To cut it short, he put up my salary a few quid a month, it was enough to pay off some of my debts. I still wasn't earning as much as a good PR girl. 'You can't leave me,' he says, and I remember the tone of his voice, it was that which struck me dumb, as if *I* had treated *him* badly.

All those years he had been trying to get into bed with me. Particularly when we went on trips. I never would. Partly because I didn't go for him much, and partly because it was a question of self-respect. It was more, it was *survival*. I couldn't let him take me over entirely. He owned my working self, but as for the rest . . . you are still wondering why I stayed with him? I remember you asked me, why stay with him, when you could earn four times the salary? The point is – I fitted that job of his like a . . . I and the job had grown up together . . . I had *made* that job, made him. He knew I wouldn't be able to give it up. He knew that in some funny way we stood and fell together . . . we matched, his talents and mine, we were a team. But he got rich, did you know? He was a millionaire. Typically he used to say, what's a million these days? And I wasn't going to say, If it's nothing, then give me a little of it. *Pride.* Okay, okay, sometimes I do wonder about that . . . but I think what I felt was, if I can stand this I can stand anything. I felt strong . . . I felt indestructible.

You did think I slept with him, didn't you? Everyone did. He made sure everyone did. He'd speak of me in a certain way, he'd put on that smile . . . if there was a big do, a first night or something, he'd take me in on his arm, and make sure everyone noticed. Caesar and his mistress. I went along with it, but I'd give him a look – and he understood all right. It was a battle, a fight to the death. I was saying, All right, but you and I know the truth. I'm not your woman and never shall be.

That went on for years. And then they offered me the job I have now and that coincided with Caesar deciding he'd had enough, time to put his feet up.

And all these years I've been thinking, you old goat, you little gauleiter, but I never slept with you.

And there I was sitting opposite old Marie and suddenly I realized she had forgotten all about it and didn't care. And that made me feel . . . I felt that I was collapsing inside, somewhere. It had been so important to me.

But at least during the lunch I understood what had happened . . . his kids were still small when I finished working for Caesar. But as they grew up they would hear him talking about me, in that proprietary way of his. Robert would have got the idea. Meanwhile I was going from strength to strength. I'm very *visible*, you know. When I was working for him it was one thing – everyone had to think his Girl Friday slept with him. But for a long time now he'd have good reason to boast about me. If you are wondering, But where did Robert get the idea about little walks in the park and tea at the Ritz, well, God knows. But he's a dear sweet lovely boy, he's nice, I mean nice in himself, he's a romantic, and so he would think that little strolls in the park and tea at the Ritz are part of the perfect love affair.

He wrote me love letters. He obviously copied them from some pattern letters. Or perhaps he got them out of a novel. I was absolutely *wowed* by them, they were like something from the eighteenth century, well perhaps they were. I'd wait a few days and then send him a couple of tickets to a play or a first night. I'd see him there with a girl, and then it was with my daughter Sonia. Do you remember her? She's beautiful. Yes, all right I can say it now ... she's like me when I was young. And *that* is the point.

Robert started taking her out regularly. I thought nothing of it. I was *busy*. I've only just realized how hard I've worked. Why did I have to, what is it all about, okay, I had to work myself silly when I had to support the children, but even when they are off my hands ... if you can call it that, none of them are ever off our hands these days, but at least they wouldn't starve if you said, enough, that's it, I've had it, don't expect any more from me – do you know one reason I would never say that? Because I wouldn't want to be as mean as Caesar, that's why.

Then, about a year ago, Marie rings me, worldly-wise, you know, and she says, 'What do you think about our Robert and your Sonia? They're getting married. We told him, you are too young, but of course none of them listen.'

I'm sure you've already worked it all out. Robert has always wanted to be Caesar the Second. *But*. He's not ambitious, you see. He doesn't know what ambition is. He works nicely in that advertising office, and dreams about being Caesar, but he doesn't make the connection somewhere ... you need to kill yourself working, or get someone else to kill themselves working for you ... he's too nice to be successful, do you see? But if he can get his father's mistress then he's half-way there.

Are you wondering how much of this my Sonia sees? Not much. She thinks I was Caesar's mistress and hates me for it. Once I said to her, Sonia, you two children and I were stuck together in two rooms until you were twenty.

You know I didn't have men – where would I have put them? What about those trips, she says, catching me out. I said Sonia, I was so tired every night often enough I used to fall into bed with all my clothes on . . . well, actually I did have the occasional little fling, when I had the energy, which wasn't often. But that has nothing to do with her. I understood something . . . she's never worked hard in her life. She doesn't know what working hard means. She doesn't know what it means being so tired you're scared to even let go half an inch, because if you did everything would fall to pieces. And she will never know because Robert looks after her like a precious kitten that will never grow up. He must think that is how his father looked after me. He's so decent that it would never enter his head to think otherwise. Caesar was a sweet kind father-figure, and so that's what he's going to be too.

To cut it short . . .

The wedding was last Saturday. We had six hundred guests. All of show business, television, radio, theatre, everything, on Caesar's side a bit reminiscent, because he's been retired for so long.

And there *we* were, Marie, mother of the bridegroom, Caesar, father of the bridegroom, Sonia's daddy – but he's always been a bit noises-off, not that it's his fault, and me, mother of the bride.

And when it came to photographs . . . no, wait, here's the nitty-gritty. Robert suddenly came forward and took charge. Suddenly I saw him as Caesar. Do you remember that deadly quiet bloody-mindedness, that determination, smiling all the time but no one was going to get in his way? That was Robert, all of last Saturday afternoon. It was absolutely essential he get a photograph of himself and Sonia, with me and Caesar standing on either side, and then a picture of us standing behind them, and then sitting in front – and so on, over and over. It was embarrassing.

Daddy and his famous mistress, and Daddy's son and the mistress as she used to be. All afternoon people were saying to me. God *darling*, but your daughter's *exactly* as you used to look.

Well, I kept giving Caesar looks, the way I used to, but he didn't know what was going on. I swear when some men retire they just give up all their *nous* – I swear, in the old days, he would have seen it all, even if he wouldn't admit it. What he did *not* see was that all of his *awful* ruthless single-mindedness, I came, I saw, I conquered, was there in his son, but focused on just one pathetic thing, that he should marry daddy's mistress.

And I felt more and more . . . that I didn't exist. Do you understand?

Well. It was ever such a *gemütlich* ceremony, it was a wonderful party, a good time was had by all, and when the happy couple went off to Venice, my treat, my daughter gave me a look of pure triumph, though God knows what she thinks she's triumphing about. And he, that *sweet* boy, he kissed me, the sort of kiss a lover gives you, goodbye for ever.

And the point is, this is the point, this is the absolutely *bloody* point . . . there is no way I could ever say to anyone, and I hardly dare think it, in case I come out with it by mistake, no, I was not Caesar's mistress, never, I never so much as kissed him, because that would be the whole basis of that sweet boy's life *gone*. The whole thing – focusing on Sonia, cutting out all her other suitors, marrying her publicly in front of his father's world and mine, treating the girl like a prize puppy – all *nothing*, based on nothing at all.

Nada.

And there's no one I can talk to about it, no one I can tell . . . except you. Well, darling, do the same for you some time.

Among the Roses

Regent's Park on a warm Saturday afternoon. With the crowds of people strolling among the roses went Myra, a middle-aged lady from Harrow, who had an expert's book on roses in her bag. Two years ago, inspired by these gardens, she had bought a rose called 'Just Joey'. This charmer had done well, and she meant to choose another. There was no greater pleasure than this, wandering through roses and deciding, I'll have you . . . no, you . . . no, perhaps . . . She had already made the circuit from the main gates with their flourishes of gold on ornamental black iron, portals to pleasure, to the right past the bird-loaded lake with the willows on one side and rose beds on the other, across Queen Mary's Rose Garden itself, and around to the left through lawns and shrubs where you crossed the long path going up to the fountain, then to the left again and by the café, and then between the beds full of tempters to where she had started. Now she was about to make another round.

As she set off, she stopped again, staring. About twenty paces in front of her, her back to her, walked a tall young woman who was striking not only because of the strident scarlet and yellow dress she wore. The dress was too tight, and emphasized a body that managed to be thin and lumpy at the same time, because of big buttocks and prominent shoulders. Myra at once felt a much too familiar anguish, which she chose to ascribe to the tactlessness that permitted that dress on that body. With a bit of luck she wouldn't turn around ... Myra knew exactly the discontented look she would see if this woman were to turn and show her bold, highly coloured face. This was her daughter, Shirley, whom she hadn't seen for three years.

What was she doing here? The last place! Flower gardens were not her style at all, let alone being by herself. Shirley was never alone, she hated it.

Myra set herself in motion again, adjusting her pace to her daughter's. Shirley was going slow, and looking at the roses. Wonders would never cease! And then Myra saw something that made her exclaim softly at the expectedness, the aptness, of it. Shirley had slipped a little pair of scissors from a pocket and was cutting off a rose on a long stem. She did not even glance around to see who had noticed her – and others besides Myra had; but her buttocks and back had a characteristic sullen defiance about them. Well, you haven't changed, Myra silently addressed Shirley. Then she thought, but perhaps she has, she must have! – for she was sure that rose had been cut to put in a pot and make roots. She did not know why she was sure. Shirley into gardening! Was it likely?

Three years before there had been a quarrel, in Myra's garden. Shirley had come especially to quarrel with her mother. She chose the moment Myra was standing in her boots and waterproof hat in her rainy garden, doing her April pruning, to stand with her hands on her hips and tell her mother she was a boring old frump who didn't care about anybody, but only her roses. If she, Shirley, thought she was going to end up like her mother, then ... It went on and on, while Myra stood listening to Shirley standing there with her hands on her round hips, her big knees showing under a short ugly dress, her face scarlet with rage – and thought she looked like the common little bitch she was. The rain splashed all around Myra while she tried to think of something to say, but then Shirley went squelching back out of the garden, and slammed out of the house.

Myra had not bothered to get in touch after that. The truth was, she was glad of the excuse not to see her. She liked Lynda, her other (her real!) daughter. Since she was born, Shirley had been nothing but trouble. Nothing done for her was ever right, nothing she did succeeded. At school she was clever but lazy and did not like her teachers. She left, without exams. She got one job after another but nothing was good enough. At nineteen she married a man Myra liked, a kindly soul Myra knew her daughter would eat up. ('She'll have him for supper the first night!' she told her husband.) But Shirley left this man and married again, a real toughie who prided himself on giving as good as he got. He was a builder's merchant, made money, took Shirley for holidays to Spain, bought her clothes. Myra believed her daughter well-matched and well-satisfied. Then, one day, on a remorseful impulse, she drove across London to visit her. No answer from the front door, so she went to the back and there, through the window of the kitchen, saw Shirley having it off on the kitchen table with some man certainly not her husband, who lifted his face, saw her and let out a yell. Up came Shirley's face, red and sweaty, and then the two let out shouts of laughter, and Shirley jumped naked off the table and screamed that her mother was spying on her. Myra had gone off home, told no one, not even her husband. Then Shirley arrived in her garden a few days later to quarrel.

She did not want to see Shirley now, but she continued

to follow her, making sure there were people between them on the path. Curiosity. Shirley not only hated plants and gardens, but the country as well, where she sulked till she could get back into town. She claimed she loathed Nature except (wink, wink) for a little of what you fancy, said she thought people who gardened were stupid and boring, and that went for her sister too. Yet here she was.

Just before the round rose garden that was framed in its garlands, Shirley turned off left and stood brooding in front of a rose Myra herself rather fancied. It was called 'L'Oreal Trophy'. A tall rose and 'luxurious in habit' as the growers would certainly describe it, the blooms were all shades of creamy pink to apricot – rose pink, and pink flame and dusky pink – no end to the sunset colours you could see there, and the buds were perfect, apricot, tightly furled. The flowers had a luminous shimmer, as if they made their own light. By this time next year the plant would be in Myra's garden. And in Shirley's?

Myra went on up into the round garden and sat on a bench where she could see the entrance. Soon Shirley came in, and Myra's heart hurt at the sight of that face, every bit as discontented as she had expected. But now it was sad, too . . . For the thousandth time she wondered, as parents do, at the difference in children. Born different! Different from the first breath. Lynda, the elder daughter, was always, from the moment she emerged, a pleasant soul, who had grown up giving no one any trouble, had gone easily to school, doing neither well nor badly, had had likeable boyfriends and married the best of them, and now lived the same kind of life her mother did, with two children, a boy and a girl. When the two women were together, Myra and Lynda, ample, slow, calm-eyed, people knew at once they were mother and daughter, but no one had ever at once thought Shirley was Myra's daughter or Lynda's sister. Where had Shirley come from then? She didn't look like her father either, and wasn't like him in nature.

If Shirley turned her head she could see her mother. She stood just inside the garden on the path, extravagant loops of roses behind her, looking alone and lonely, her big shoulders hunched forward, her shining black hair making licks down her red cheeks, her short gaudy skirts showing big knees. This ugly woman was attractive to men, always had been, even as a small girl. Men were looking at her now.

Shirley went to the round central bed, which was like a gigantic posy crammed tight with another pinky creamy orangey rose, this time called 'Troika'. Myra was not going to buy that, it lacked subtlety, did not have the unearthly shimmer to it. And now, incredibly, Shirley did it again. She slid the scissors from her pocket and snipped off a rose on a long sturdy stem. This found its way to the other in her bag. Had anyone seen? Shirley wouldn't care! She'd bluff it out. You imagined it, she'd say with her sulky affronted air. Call the police then! Challenged with: Suppose everyone did it? – she'd reply, triumphant, with: But they don't, do they?

Myra decided for the hundredth time she didn't want any more of Shirley. She got up from her bench, not bothering about being noticed, and walked past 'Troika' on the other side of the bed to her daughter, and out of the garden to where the miniature roses were.

Suddenly it occurred to her: perhaps she came here hoping she'd run into me? She knows I come here a lot.

And indeed, as she turned away left, away from the roses, she heard noisy feet running.

'Hello, Mum,' said Shirley. 'Fancy seeing you.'

'How are you?' Myra cautiously inquired.

'Oh, mustn't complain.'

'You've taken to gardening, then?'

'It's beginning to get to me, believe it or not. We moved, did you know? It's got a big garden. I suppose you don't know. Well, let bygones be, what do you say?'

'You and Brian?' inquired Myra carefully. Brian was the builder's merchant.

'Oh not him, we split up. And good riddance. He beat me, Mum!' said Shirley, and laughed. Full of resentment, full of admiration. That meant he had left her, Myra decided.

'Are you divorced then?'

'Yes, it came through just after Christmas. And now I've got a really nice one. You'd like him, I know that.'

'Have I met him?' inquired Myra, drily, thinking of the naked man she'd seen through the kitchen window, whose voice she had heard, yelling with laughter. But it seemed Shirley had forgotten the incident, or at least that there had been a man Myra might remember.

'You couldn't have met him. I only met him myself last autumn.'

'You're going to marry him, then?'

'Christ no, what's the point? No, twice is enough. We'll live together. We hit it off though. Made for each other.'

'That's good,' said Myra. She noted that as usual with this daughter she was watching every word she said. Shirley reacted unpredictably, could be rude, explosive, sullen, even pleasant – but one never knew. Myra felt that half her life she had been behaving as if Shirley were a minefield, and she was running across it.

The two women walked on in silence. The lawn with squirrels running about it. The shrubby hillside. Where the long path up to the fountain crossed this one, Myra hesitated, letting Shirley choose, but Shirley decided to walk straight on, and not to go up to the fountain. Myra meekly went with her. As always.

At the café Myra wondered whether to say, 'Would you like a cup of tea?' but did not dare.

On they went, and for the second time Myra was walking slowly along the path where beds of roses stood on either side. Shirley stopped. Myra stopped. 'How do you prune these things?' asked Shirley.

'Well, that's easy enough,' said Myra, and she bent over the low railing, ready to show how. 'You must prune to an outside bud,' she began, and was going on, when it struck her. Shirley might be – everything she was, but she wasn't stupid. If she was taking cuttings – stealing cuttings – then she must know how to prune. She would have learnt out of a book, as Myra had. Myra straightened herself and said, 'Would you like to come over one day and I'll show you on my roses at home?'

'That's an idea. Yes, I'd like that,' said Shirley.

'When would you like to come? The weekend? The thing is, Dad won't be there, he's off fishing this weekend.'

'We'll be by ourselves, then?'

'You wouldn't like to bring your new – the one you're living with now?'

'Oh, him! What for? No, I'd just like to see you, I've been missing you, believe it or not.'

'Well, that's nice.'

'He goes on nature rambles,' said Shirley, 'every bloody weekend.'

'Then I'll be a fishing widow and you'll be a nature ramble widow,' dared Myra, smiling – as she knew – with nervousness.

'Why do you put up with it?' demanded Shirley, suddenly full of furious black resentment that positively scorched her mother. 'You always put up with everything. Why do you?'

'But I don't mind. Why should I? Does us good to be apart the occasional weekend.'

'You always put up with everything,' shrieked Shirley. 'I've never heard you stand up to him, never.'

'Stand up to him?' said Myra, amazed. 'Why should I need to do that?'

'Oh God,' said Shirley. 'I can't believe it. I simply cannot believe . . .' She stopped, evidently remembering that she had just made up with her mother and did not want to quarrel again. At least, not yet. 'Oh well, it takes all sorts,' she conceded, as agreeably as was possible to her.

'Yes, it certainly does,' said Myra with a sigh. But she changed the sigh into a cough, for fear it would set Shirley off again.

*S*torms

In Frankfurt they told me there was a metre of water in the streets of London. These floods had come just after the great storm of wind that blew down so many of London's trees. When I came out of the airport building in the late afternoon to find a taxi, the pastel-tinted, flying skies made everything under them seem small and temporary, and people's faces had a look of mourning. I had a cough and a bad throat and should not have flown at all: my ears had taken punishment and I was half-deaf. I stood in the taxi queue with one eye on those unreliable skies, and wondered if the storm damage in my garden I had left two days ago had been cleared up yet, and if the floods had made things even worse. Because my mind was at odds with itself, being full of storm winds and waters and the results of cough medicines, when my turn came I hesitated: the small bobbing man in tweeds and that kind of cap you can pull down over the ears – tied now into a flat checked pancake across the top of the head – seemed more like a countryman at a market than a London taxi driver. 'Are you going to get in, then?' he asked, and I got in and said I lived in West Hampstead up the hill from Mill Lane. This formula is at once recognized by every

London taxi driver, but he replied that he did not drive in London, and this remark seemed part of my general delirium. I joked that I had never driven with a phantom taxi driver before. He was silent, his head half turned to me, listening, then gruffly said that he was no phantom, and there was a Mill Lane near where he lived, and how did he know I didn't mean that? So he was a bit deaf. Just as I was, that evening. He began questioning me about where I lived: he did not want to admit he didn't know what I said every taxi driver knew and he asked if, in my opinion, the best way to go was this way or that, for he always liked to learn other people's routes. It was hard to hear him, for my ears hurt badly, and I was leaning forward. This gave me a look of willing attention, but I had decided I'd rather he didn't talk at all, for he did not seem at his ease, but drove like grandfather being given his turn to drive the family car on a Sunday afternoon. He gripped the wheel and peered over it and muttered about other drivers' behaviour, and exclaimed, 'Did you see that? Did you see what he did then?' I thought: Well, better be philosophical, this is one of the journeys you are going to be pleased to see the end of. We were taking the slow roads in, not the quick side roads drivers use who know an area. What was this man who did not drive in London doing here? Should he be driving at all? Meanwhile we talked: I leaned forward: he half-turned his head. First of all, of course, about the big storm of three nights ago. He, at the bottom of his house, had slept through it and woke to find the trees down in the street and his garden shed's roof gone. I told him how it had been with me, sitting up in my bed at the top of the house, having been woken suddenly about two. The sky kept changing completely, one minute black with the glimmer of sheet lightning far away across London, and then clear and starry, and the stars had a rinsed look because of the clear, washed air, then black again, and the temperature was changing, stuffy and warm and then suddenly cold, then warm again, while the trees, particularly the big ash at the bottom of the garden, were boiling and thrashing about and everything in the house was rattling and banging, and the roof seemed about to shake itself off. All the lights were on in the houses, for people were watching and waiting, but they went out when the power failed, and you could see for miles across the blacked-out city, with one remote twinkle of light far away in the dark. You don't often see London without its lights, the last time was the big strike in the seventies, but I noticed then that it is never really black dark, light comes from somewhere: surely the candles and torches glimmering in every house are not enough to make the soft ghost's light? It was not until I remarked that my cat had not wanted me up there, had tried to get me to move downstairs, and had gone down himself to a safe place in the heart of the house, that he became interested. 'You should have done what your cat told you to do,' he said, 'they know better than we do.'

'I'm still alive,' I said.

'Yes, but you never know what might have happened.'

'I wouldn't have missed that sight for anything.'

'Yes, and all those branches flying about and the tiles crashing . . . did you notice where the cat put himself? Then that's the safest place in the house. You should remember that. It was under a beam somewhere, wasn't it? Then that's it – they know. That's where people put themselves in the blitz, under the stairs or under a good strong beam.'

I asked if he had a cat, but he said, 'No, a dog. I like a good dog, a dog's a friend to you.'

'But so is a cat,' I said.

A pause. 'I lost my dog,' he said, or half-shouted back at

me – this conversation continued with difficulty. His voice was gruff and even angry. 'Yes, it was a month ago. I had to take him to the vet, you see . . .' The way he said this told me, This hurts, keep off, so I only said that I sympathized because a few weeks ago I had had to take a special cat to the vet, when he became too ill to live. I missed him, I said. I kept expecting him to walk in at the door.

'You do miss them. I don't expect to get used to not having my dog with me, not for a good time yet.'

I sat back in the seat and looked at the fallen trees, their roots in the air like hands that had tried to grip the soil to keep them upright, but failed. The soil packed among the roots was already being washed out. Everywhere were broken branches, and the signs of recent high water, tidemarks of rubble and leaves and twigs. It was becoming dark. October: the clocks would soon go back for the winter.

When we came to the Westway it was solid with cars, and he said he had never seen the Westway like this before – thus casually making his claim to being a London driver, after all. Not usual, this, to have to slow down on Westway, and then crawl along and then have to stop altogether. We agreed that the seas of water had been too much for drains, or for the electricity or gas pipes, and so some roads had had to close. We crawled . . . stopped . . . crawled. How much he hated London, he said violently, and I leaned forward again. He had been so happy, moving to a small town not far from London. London was not what it was, it was full of people he didn't think were Londoners at all. And they talked in a funny way. Only last week he had bought a newspaper from a shop he remembered from before he left, and a boy behind the counter, just a youngster he was, had said, 'There you go, then.' And he had said, 'How do you know I'm going anywhere?' 'It stands to reason you're going somewhere, grandad.' 'Well, what's that to you, if I am? Do you talk to your grandad like that?'

'It's a manner of speaking,' I said.

'It's not my manner,' he said. 'And, if you ask me, they have no manners at all, not one of them.'

And now I began to tell him how much I enjoyed London, from that ridiculous need to make other people like what you like. It was like a great theatre, I said; you could watch what went on all day, and sometimes I did. You could sit for hours in a café or on a bench and just watch. Always something remarkable, or amusing . . . and the parks, I said, Regent's Park, Hampstead Heath: you could never get tired of them. Here he remarked that the parks had all been closed because of the storm, so many trees had come crashing down, it was enough to make you cry, he said, he had seen people stand at their gates crying their eyes out because of their trees lying smashed and broken . . . I was understanding that this voice was full of grief, it was not the grumbling grievance of an old man, no, this was sorrow, and it was what I had been hearing, seeing, since I got into his cab. Was all this because of his dog? Surely not!

I went on talking about London, partly because I enjoy sharing what I feel about this city, but also because I wanted to find out what the mystery was I felt in him. Perhaps this wasn't his taxi, and he was driving it for someone else, for some reason? Or he had stopped driving, but had had to go back to it? Or something in his own small town was making it hard for him to drive there?

He was silent as I talked about London, but then allowed it had its advantages – or, rather, once had had advantages, but now nothing would make him leave his own little town, a country town, where there wasn't all this noise and rush.

On the Westway I had suggested he avoid Kilburn

High Street, always crammed, but it turned out that West End Lane was as bad. 'What are all these people doing here at this time of the evening?' he wanted to know, clutching his wheel and glaring this way and that. 'It's past rush hour.'

'Well,' I said, 'they might be off to the theatre, or coming home after having supper in town.'

'They'd do better to eat in their own homes, what are they going to get in a restaurant better than they get at home? Gadding about and spending money, never staying quiet and thinking their own thoughts.' His voice was full of hurt.

When I suggested a short cut round the back streets he took it, and we went along faster, through streets still full of litter and blown leaves. Here and there a tree was down, or slanting, and branches had been ripped off. Along the strip of scrubby ground that drops to the railway lines the storm had not done much damage. I commented on this, saying I was pleased for the sake of the animals and birds who live there, and he said it was a poor state of affairs when animals have to take refuge in towns because the countryside is so hard on them.

Outside my house he had to double park. Having put my case down on the pavement he came forward to me and stood close. His head was on a level with mine. In the half dark of the street I saw he was a gingery whiskery little man, with warm brown eyes full of need. He gripped my hand urgently and said, 'You see, driving like this all day, it numbs your mind, it dulls you, and you can't think the thoughts you ought to have in your mind.' Gripping my hand he turned me around so that the light from the street lamp fell on to my face and he could see it, and his hand was strong, and warm, a kind hand, with nothing of the wild dislocation that was in his voice, matching torn trees and flying skies. 'I'm not a cab driver by rights,' he said.

'I was a musician. I had my own group – you'd know the name if I told you, that is, if you know music. But then . . . you see, it was a woman, that's what happened, a woman. All my troubles began with her. Her father and her brothers were taxi drivers and she wanted me to be one and so for her sake that's what I did. I spent months cycling all over London learning The Knowledge – do you know what that is?'

'Of course I do. Everyone knows London taxi drivers have to pass an examination before they get a licence.'

'Yes, and it's a real exam, I can tell you, you have to know your streets, and that's The Knowledge . . . well, months I was on it, months . . . that was a long time ago and I have another wife now.' He gripped my hand even tighter and leaned forward to look into my face to make sure I was going to accept what he said. 'I don't like people,' he said. 'I like animals. They are better than we are. They are kind, not cruel, like us.' Meanwhile, a car was waiting to pass, and had given us enough time to say whatever it was we had to say. It began to hoot, persistently, like the beginning of Beethoven's Fifth. He let my hand go. 'People are ugly and stupid,' I heard, as he got into his seat. 'If you don't agree with me now, you will, you'll see, we're no good!' He gave me a wave, more like a formal but comradely salute. He drove off, a small, squashed-looking figure behind the wheel, peering over it. He had told me he was going straight back to Heathrow to pick up another fare.

_H_ er

What makes a salon? A potent hostess, or host? A house or room with sympathetic qualities? The guests? Easy to say that the recipe must be a combination of all these, until exceptions start knocking at your memory. But surely it would be generally agreed that these days we do not have salons, the paradigmatic At Homes were in the past. Everyone knows the names of the resplendent hostesses who were centres of politics and literature, in London and in Paris, and they certainly knew that their drawing-rooms were salons. Now it is possible to find out, long after the event, that a house visited innocently was really a salon, and similarly writers may find out they were part of a Movement. Did all the Bloomsburies know what they were?

To be a molecule in a literary group is expected of a writer, but not in this country. Writers often get this letter: 'What literary group do you belong to, and what does it stand for?' The reply: 'We do not have literary groups in this country, writers tend to leave London and find solitude in the countryside, dipping back into London for special occasions or in a rare fit of gregariousness.' There is no guarantee that they, too, will not find that they were part of some Movement or other, perhaps on the basis of a visit to a restaurant or an acquaintance. Certainly houses or living rooms, which do not know they are, will turn out to have been salons. Not long ago in London a couple on the fringes of diplomacy 'received' on a certain evening in every week. Invitations were not sent out, welcome guests were told, almost as an aside, that they would find food and drink, and a mix of people. These were mostly politicians and journalists, some of them attracted because of the other. To know how often titbits of information, 'leaked' secrets, careless talk, made paragraphs and even Leaders, or inspired television programmes, one would have to have been a regular. But this Salon was worth visiting, once, twice, out of curiosity about what goes on up there, in the high lands of influence, particularly when 'the country' was in a seethe about something: we tend to use this corporate word at such times.

The house was ten minutes by taxi from the House of Commons, and politicians would drop in for a few minutes, or an hour, between appointments with Duty in the House. They tended to arrive in groups. One could imagine a Member saying to another, 'Let's drop over to Mix and Match for a bite.' No one knew who made this joke first.

The reception room extended over the first floor, over-looking a small formal garden at the back, and at the front a street with a name that was a guarantee of worth. Along one wall was a buffet, and trays of drinks circled through the guests, borne by smiling girls. When the politicians came in they brought with them the excitement familiar to anyone who has taken part in the organization of public events, the elation that goes with the conviction that one has power.

Their entry was like the checked rush you see at the moment the gates are swung back to admit a bull into a ring: an impetuousness halted by a stare all around to find out what Fate provided, and then on he comes, they come, to reach at once for a drink off a hovering tray. If this tray was held forward by a pretty girl, then the action of taking the glass might be accompanied by a bold or a furtive stare, even a smile that hinted at advantageous intimacies.

Innocents may imagine that Left and Right, Tories and Labour, would arrive separately, and even make exclusive groups, but no, they might arrive together and stand matily about with a look that said they felt out of bounds, off a leash: they could do as they liked, being unsupervised. There was a general effect of mix and movement, but there were more men than women, though there were some wives of diplomats, and a female journalist or two.

The two times I was there 'the country' was in an uproar, it was an issue that caused Tory and Labour confrontations in the House, every newspaper headline emphasized left–right conflict, and some of the people there, but not regular guests, were watching the politicians in case some words of enlightenment were on offer. But politics was not what they talked about. No, they gossiped, all the talk was of how Bertie had said that, or Norman let fall this, and that *she* had announced – something or other. 'He is going to see *her*, he told me, but Bernard . . .'

Journalists stood about, trying to overhear, or to catch an eye which was usually not anxious to be caught, but one might observe how a journalist slowly edged nearer to a politician, with the concentration of a sheepdog, and a moment later the politician would be neatly cut out from the group, and held isolated as the two stood glass to glass. The politician might be bestowing a few words, or his body announced that he had been trapped, but in either case, he was the giver of favours.

Then he was back in the group and a dozen glasses

made a fraternal convocation, rising as they went to the
mouths, descending between gulps, moving in gleaming
circles or ellipses with the emphases of the talk, sometimes
approaching each other, with an effect of intimacy, or
indiscretion, or even clashing . . . 'I'm so sorry', 'Sorry' . . .
and, as the trays went past, globules of glass were replaced,
and others taken in to this little separate dance which was
like a commentary on the unheard conversation.

Women politicians seldom came. There aren't many in
the House. One evening a slim dark woman entered in
the kind of dress females choose to define not themselves
but a function, a sober dark red: if it were made in
white or blue it could be a nurse's uniform, or a shop
or airport supervisor's. She seemed concerned to give
the impression that she took up less space than she did.
She did not appear to see the bunch of male politicians
who stood in the centre of the room, but preserved an
all-purpose smile, and circumvented the group until she
reached a sofa where sat a young woman journalist whom
she had expected – it was obvious – to see there. Perhaps
they had even made an arrangement to meet. At once they
began an exchange in low voices, and the journalist made
some notes, but unobtrusively. When that was done, after
perhaps ten minutes, the woman politician turned to look
over the room, which seemed full of men. The woman
journalist did the same. Both were wary, with a little look
of humour.

'They seem quite tame tonight,' commented the repre-
sentative of the *Mentor* – a right-wing paper, while she,
in fact, was rather to the left, and known for her articles
on women's affairs.

'They were pretty rowdy in the House earlier,' said the
politician. 'It's all the late nights. They get over-excited.
You can watch them getting more wrought up as the term
goes on.'

'I'm sure an early night wouldn't do any of them any harm,' said the journalist. 'I was in the House last week, for the War Dependents Allowances Debate. They struck me as being really above themselves.'

They discussed the ebullient males, boys will be boys, for some time, and then the female politician lowered her voice and talked about the difficulties of being a female politician, of whatever party. By now several women sat on the sofa and in chairs near it: a little nest of females.

The male politicians were planning to crowd off together down the stairs, putting their glasses carelessly back on the trays held out to them, and giving a last assessing look around, in case they had missed some opportunity.

One remarked, raising his voice to be heard, 'I'm proud to be serving under her, I'd say that anywhere – but . . .' and his circling glance was both roguish and aggressive, 'she must watch her step.'

'Exactly,' said another, 'if she steps out of line, don't imagine we wouldn't give her the push.'

At the time these remarks seemed like the mere froth of male conviviality, but now they tend to isolate themselves in memory: this was *her* second term of office, and she was at the height of her success.

The woman politician remarked, 'I'll give them a minute to get clear . . .' and went on to tell how any woman Member of Parliament, entering the Chamber or leaving it, no matter how they effaced themselves, could expect sexual heckling of the kind you'd expect from – 'well, schoolboys'.

'Louts on a street corner,' suggested the journalist.

'Groups of workmen on a site shouting sexual epithets after a pretty girl,' said another woman.

We all had our eyes on the men, now off down the stairs with shouts and cries of 'See you again . . .' 'Must go . . .' 'The Whip'll have our heads . . .'

'Every morning when I wake up,' said the woman politician, 'I tell myself that I've got to take it, I've got to keep cool, because you have to smile, no matter what they throw at you. You might want to hit them, but if you don't smile they go from bad to worse. It's hard, sometimes.' She spoke quietly but her smile did not come easily.

She got up, went to the window overlooking the street, came back. 'I'll give them another minute, they're waiting for taxis.

'That's one of the things I admire *her* for. She doesn't let it get to her. Well, it must get to her, but she never lets it show. She's always been attractive, she's always been a target . . . they are afraid of her now she's boss but they're so malicious about her behind her back – sometimes I can't believe what I'm hearing. Well, I'm not as tough as she is, nothing like. Sometimes I know I show what I'm feeling . . . she never does. Never.'

'At the Party Conference,' said the journalist, 'the chambermaids at the hotel told me they try never to be alone, they stick in pairs, because when *they* are drunk, anything goes.'

'Yes, I am afraid it is all a bit like a *Carry On* film.'

As the two women went out, another group of men came in, laughing, high on their success, their achievement.

The women went quickly, quietly, past them, like shadows along the wall, and the men really did not seem to see them.

*T*he *Pit*

A final sprig of flowering cherry among white lilac and yellow jonquils, in a fat white jug . . . she stuck this in judiciously, filling in a pattern that needed just so much attention. Shouting 'Spring!' the jug sat on a small table in the middle of the room.

Spring sang in the plane trees that crammed two windows along one wall. The windows of the other wall showed a sprightly blue sky. The trees, full of young leaves, were reflected in the two round mirrors set to match the windows, like portholes in the white wall. Opposite the end wall with its square of blue sky she had hung a large seascape bought for a few pounds in a street market: in it blue sea, blue sky, white spray, white clouds eternally tumbled over each other. It had been painted with a fresh and probably youthful zest by someone called Samantha.

You could think this a large room, extended into infinite variety by the weather outside, but it was small, and so was her bedroom next door. The flat comprised two adequate rooms, and here she had lived for a time.

Having completed preparations for the visit from James, the man to whom she had been married for ten years, she did not sit down, but remained standing by the little table whose surface reflected the flowers. She was giving her room a slow, hooded, prowling look, an inspection not from her viewpoint, but from his. She could not remember his ever actually having criticized her arrangements, but going off with a woman whose taste in every way was the opposite to hers surely must be considered a criticism?

She did not know why he was coming. Two years had passed since she had rung him about some message from Nancy, their daughter, about an urgent need for money. Before that, they had met for lunch, in Manchester as it happened, where she was working and he visiting. In 1980, she thought that was. This encounter had been handled by both of them as if bullets might start flying around the restaurant at a single wrong word, and the strain of it had prevented another. Before that, meetings had always been for legal reasons and policed by solicitors, or because of the children.

But when he had telephoned to say he wanted to meet her 'just to talk', what she had felt, unexpectedly, was delight, as if she were opening a present so well chosen she could feel the giver's thoughts dwelling lovingly among her own, approving her choices.

She perfectly understood the quality of this delight, its exact weight and texture, because of a smile that these days she sometimes felt arriving on her face together with thoughts of certain men. It was a rich, irresponsible, free-booter's smile, and she knew that this smile must appear on their faces when they thought of her: a smile that had nothing to do with what society might be saying at any given time, or with morality, or with the wars between men and women.

But the point was, he – her husband – had not been one of these men, for thoughts of him had been loaded with anxiety and self-doubt. Now she felt that he had been restored to her.

She stood with one capable hand among the reflections of the flowers on the shining tabletop and smiled, not bothering to look in the mirror, for she knew that just as she, meeting him, would seek – anxiously but confidently – among the dry ruins for what she remembered of a quarter of a century ago, so he would seek in her what she had been. This is how former lovers meet, when ageing, as if suffused by that secret, irrepressible smile.

Once upon a time, when young, walking along a pavement or into a room, they had never failed to see in the faces turned towards them the gratified look that comes from absolute rightness. They had been a match, a pair, flesh of an immediately recognizable category of flesh. Both good-looking, healthy, fitted to mate and beget, causing none of the secret unease that people feel when confronted by couples who can make you think only of the unhealthy or ugly offspring they are likely to produce. Sarah and James had given others pleasure that had in fact little to do with being young, handsome, healthy, and so on. No, it was because of their being flesh of one flesh. They had both been tall; she, slim, he, spare. Both were fair, he with shaggy Viking locks, she with long pale gleaming tresses. Both had very blue eyes, full of shrewd innocence. If there ever had been moments of disquiet in their early days, it was because of this: when they lay in each other's arms and looked into that other face, what they saw was so similar to what they saw in mirrors.

The woman he had married after her was large, black-haired, swarthy – a nice change, she had thought, in her bitter days. The children he and this gypsy had made between them were 'one white and one black and two khaki', as she had put it, full of shame. (Not literally 'black' of course: one was like her mother, brown and sleek and dark-eyed; one like James, pale and fair with eyes that shocked because of their blueness; and two indeterminate beings like neither.) Nice-looking children, but when these six people were all together no one need think of them as a family.

When Sarah and James were together, with their two children, they were four of a kind, blue-eyed, blond Northern Europeans, so different from the majority of the world's people that you had to think this was some kind of a rare and threatened race and you were being privileged to see perfect representatives of it. She had not seen things like this then, but later she did, confronted with Rose and the new family.

The two children were now, of course, more than grown up. One was in Boston. This was Nancy with her husband and children. The son was on some island in the Pacific investigating the ways of fish. She did not often see either of them, or her grandchildren. She was pretty sure this was because of the divorce happening when it did, when they were ten and eleven. Protecting themselves, they had separated inwardly not only from their father, who had betrayed them for the new family, but from her, the innocent party. They had become cautious, sparing of affection, self-doubting, and critical. Of her. Unjust! But these days she never used, or thought, words like justice, or happiness.

When her Viking husband had left her for the siren-voiced, histrionic, over-colourful Rose, she had – of course! – been devastated. Literally. She fell apart. Well, women did. She was for a time poisoned with bitterness, she could not believe that her husband, her *friend*, had so treated her. Oh no, it was not possible: she confronted him with the impossibility of it, the indignant innocence of her gaze demanding an explanation she could acknowledge. She drank too much. Then she stopped drinking. She coped well and sensibly with the two sensible and over-cautious children who, like her, protected a calloused place.

But all that had gone away, seemed to belong to some other time, even some other woman.

Now she felt herself connected, not with that vulnerable discarded woman, but with herself as a girl, before she had met him.

Deliverance from weakness had not happened quickly. Five years after the divorce, at a party, he had stared at her, as if unable to believe what his eyes and senses told him, that this was – still – his wife, with whom he had lived for ten years. The tears spilled down his face, and he exclaimed, 'But Sarah, what happened?' At which she had been so angry she spat at him (astonishing herself as well as him – it was behaviour she associated with gypsy women, never her moderate self) and turned her back on him and left the party, weeping. But other women had told her that on unexpectedly meeting former husbands, these men would also exclaim, genuinely startled, 'But what happened?' As if their delinquency was something not only surprising to them, but not really their responsibility at all, rather the result of some ineluctable fate.

For a while, she had raged over what she had then seen as the lying sentimentality of 'But what happened?' Had raged briefly, because one did *not* permit self-indulgence in useless emotion. And then had forgotten, it had all gone away, and when she thought of him, not often these days, what she saw was the blue innocence of that look of his, reflecting the candour and honesty that she had first loved in him, qualities she prized above all others.

Now she lived in her two adequate rooms. In the same town as he did – but that was chance. Because of her work she had lived in Paris, New York, various towns in England, always moving, and good at moving. She never felt she lived in one place more than another. She was a personal secretary in a big oil firm.

But her husband had left her for that other house where he had lived, not moving at all, with his new family. Not always contentedly, as she knew. But she did not now care about all that. He had made his bed, and she genuinely hoped it was a good one. She did not care, one way or the other. Not to care, that was the great, the unexpected, the miraculous deliverance. What a lot of nonsense it all was, the anguish, and the suffering, and the lying awake at nights weeping! What a waste of time.

And now when she was free of him, James was coming to see her.

His footsteps approached. Rapidly. Lightly. He was taking two steps at a time up the stairs, then he knocked, and was in, standing just inside the door and looking at her.

Knowing exactly how they must look to each other, they frowned with the effort of re-creating younger selves in what they were actually seeing. Their eyes met without difficulty, and did not disengage because of confusion, pain, guilt. Perhaps they had not really seen each other since the separation.

What she was looking at was an elderly Viking, his shaggy locks, like hers, tarnished with silver. He was much burned by sun, wind, so there must have been a very recent walking holiday somewhere. His handsome face was thin, all crags and ravines. He seemed to have dried out, as she seemed to herself to be dry and light, time dragging moisture out of her, like a sun.

His acute gaze now left her, and rested on the flowers . . . a small table where she took her meals . . . a gas fire with a light armchair beside it . . . a shelf of books . . . the tumultuous blue and white seascape. Then he approached the blue square of the end window, with his fast light high

step that had been the first thing in him to delight her. It
still did. At the window he looked downward into a scene
of back gardens, birds, trees, fences loaded with creepers,
children's climbing frames, cats stretched out absorbing
sunlight. Family life ... He was scrutinizing it with a
small dry smile she knew well. Then he stepped quickly
to one window in the side wall, and then the other: the
same view from both; a quiet street lined with parked
cars, plane trees, an old woman sitting on a bench.

This was the second floor. In summer the trees were
like towns full of birds, and she stood there watching
them. He turned about, and stood checked in his need
to step off to somewhere else in this room. He was
used to rooms where one might walk about, take a
short stroll. But there was nowhere else. He was feeling
confined.

'I suppose you are wondering what I'm doing here?'
he said hastily, but then went red, because it sounded
conventional, though she had not taken it like that.

'Well, yes, I did wonder,' she said agreeably, and sat herself down near the flowers. She at once became conscious
of how she must look, posed near these flowers she had
bought because of pleasure at his coming, and she moved
quickly to the armchair near the gas fire. It was a chair that
made one sit up straight. She sat there lightly and erectly,
and looked at him. And sighed. She heard the sigh, and
saw his quick conscious look when he heard it, and it was
her turn to blush.

He sat down near one of the windows and beyond him
a plane tree shook with the visitations of birds. He looked
as if he might leap to his feet and be off again. A hunted
man, he frowned, and put his lean brown hand to his face,
but then let it drop and sighed too, and sat back in his chair
to face her.

'There isn't a reason really,' he announced. 'It began

to seem to me so wrong, that we didn't even meet occasionally.'

She merely smiled, agreeing that they had not met only because of some whim or oversight.

'We were together all that time . . . the children . . .' He shrugged, giving up, and looked straight at her, inviting aid.

She could, she supposed, ask after his children, his other family. But there was no point in his coming, no point in all this upset and adjustment and sighing and excitement if all they did was to exchange pretexts for not talking. Besides, she knew how they all were, his family: a good friend of hers remained a good friend of his, and reported what went on. Not like a spy, but like a friend. Once she had needed to know; recently she had listened as if to news from a household that did not much concern her.

He half got up, but sat down again, seeing there was nowhere to move to. 'You don't have much space up here,' he remarked. It sounded like a reproach, and he again reddened.

'But I don't need much space.' And now this, she felt, could be taken as a reproach, and she made an irritable gesture – too irritable for what was happening, full of elderly impatience at the trivial. 'I didn't mean . . .' she exclaimed carefully, 'what I meant was, I *don't* need much room, now the children are grown up. Nancy and Martin hardly need their own rooms any longer!'

Suddenly he seemed tired. She knew why. The house he now lived in was large, full of rooms in which one might take a little stroll. But it was of course always needing repairs the way houses did, and it was shabby, because it was a much used family house, exploding with the four children and their friends. It pulsated with people, noise, music, telephones ringing, loud voices – Rose's, particularly – singing, a dog barking, doorbells, the drone of vacuum cleaners. Family life. The oldest child was fifteen, the youngest, nine. In front of James was at least ten years, probably much more, of finding a good deal of money for education. He was a business consultant. He had not wanted to be one. But that was what he had become when, needing a lot of money for the new marriage, he had given up his previous career as an expert in electronics for the aircraft industry and for boats. That was what he had enjoyed.

Everything he did now, where he lived and how, was because he had fallen in love with Rose, her own opposite in every way, and gone off with her. And things would go on as they were now, they would have to, for years and years. He was fifty-three. He would grow old in Rose's service. That was what he had chosen. If you could use a word like 'choose'.

She was two years older than he.

She said, 'I decided to retire this year. They asked me to stay on, but I don't want to.'

And now his whole person was momentarily full of the energy of words not spoken, words of aggressive inquiry, if not reproach. It was he who had arranged her very good job with the oil firm. He knew – since the man she had worked for all these years was a friend – that pressure had been put on her to be more than a personal secretary. They had offered her all kinds of better jobs. But she had not wanted to become ambitious and sink her life in the firm's. She had found her own life more interesting, and had been careful to guard it. But had she accepted, money would have been much less tight. She knew of course that James had been critical of her for being content to be a mere secretary, and this quite apart from the money side of it.

She said, 'I don't need very much money now. I can do as I please.'

'Lucky Sarah,' he said, suddenly emotional.

'Yes, I think so.'

'There is no way, no way at *all* that I could *not* have gone off with Rose,' he said unexpectedly. Unexpectedly to him: but she knew this was why he had come. He had to say this! Not as a justification. Not as a plea. He needed to explain some absolute, some imperative, that she – his first wife – must acknowledge. He was asking for justice. From her!

'No, I know,' she said judicially.

'It was like . . .' He hesitated, and not from delicacy, or wanting to spare her, or himself, but because of the astonishment even now: his face was contracted with the effort of coming to terms with what he remembered. 'I don't understand it,' he said. 'I didn't then. I never have. I could even say I didn't like her particularly . . .' His look at her insisted she must not take this as disloyalty to Rose, or an excuse.

'I know,' she said again.

'It was because . . . but I simply had to . . . it was like being carried away by a . . .'

Now she made a sharp irritable gesture, meaning *That's enough*. But he did not see it, or if he did, decided to ignore it.

'Have you ever thought, Sarah . . . we are so alike, we two . . .'

She nodded.

His eyes had filled with tears, and it was because of his bewilderment.

'From one extreme to the other,' he said. 'We never had to explain anything, did we? We always understood . . . but with her, it's like a wrong turning in a foreign country, and I don't know the language.' A silence. 'The dark and the light of it,' he said. A silence. 'I am not saying I regret it. You don't regret what you couldn't help. Or if you do it's a waste of time.'

'Of course not,' she agreed.

And now he did get up and stand before her, hands dangling, but with their characteristic look of being on the alert and ready for anything. An embrace? But he went instead to the end window, whose blue square now showed a fat and cherubic cloud, white with gold and fawn shadows. He looked at the cloud, over the disordered back gardens.

'What are you going to do, Sarah?'

'I want to travel.'

'But you're always on the move. Every time I hear of you, you're somewhere else,' he said, with the short laugh that means suppressed envy.

'Yes, I've been lucky. It's been a lovely job, thanks to you. But they say elderly women get restless feet, and that's what I've got.'

'Not only women,' he said, but shut off the complaint with, 'Are you going to visit Nancy and Martin?'

'Briefly.'

He looked an inquiry.

'I would not describe us as a close family,' she said, and he reddened again.

'Well, I think perhaps we are. Rose is good at that, making a family, I mean.'

At this, resentment nearly overwhelmed her. She knew he had never understood what it had been like for her, the years of bringing up the children without him. He never would. She maintained a smiling silence. But now she felt at a distance from him, because of his not under-standing.

'Anyway, it wasn't such a bad thing,' he said. 'They saw all those different places with you moving about so much, and they were in different schools and fit in anywhere.'

'Citizens of the world,' she said dryly. 'That's what they are, all right.'

He could have taken this up, pressing his point, which was necessary to him. But she stopped it with, 'I shall begin by going on walking tours here. In this country first. I mean, real long ones, all summer . . .'

'Ah yes,' he said energetically, 'there's nothing like it.'

'And then I shall go walking in France and Germany, well, everywhere I can in Europe. Norway . . .'

'Ah yes,' he said, restless, his feet moving as if ready to set off then and there.

Rose did not like walking.

'Around the world,' she said. 'Why not?' And she laughed, her whole body, her face, alive with delight at the thought of it, setting off free as a bird . . . No, that was wrong, birds were not free, they had to obey all kinds of patterns and forces – free as only a human being can be. Though, probably, life being what it was, free only for a short, treasured time before something or other happened. Free to walk, stop, make friends, wander, change her mind, sit all day on a mountainside if she felt like it, watching clouds . . . She had actually forgotten that he stood there, watching her, smiling his appreciation of her.

'Sarah,' he said, in a low intimate voice, with the thrill of recklessness in it, 'why can't we two go off again somewhere, this summer, soon . . .'

The two smiled at each other, as if their faces were a few inches apart on a pillow. Then she heard herself sigh, and she saw the energy go out of him.

'But why not, Sarah?' he urged.

This meant that what Olive had told her was true. Rose was having an affair, and he did not feel bound to be loyal.

'You mean, Rose wouldn't mind?'

The thought of how much Rose would mind, and how she would show it, was obviously like a blow to the back of his knees, for he sank down abruptly, and stared, not at her, Sarah, but at the cloud, which now seemed sculptured out of honey-coloured stone.

'Or you wouldn't tell her?' she persisted.

Going off with her on a walking tour was an impulse. He had not thought of it before he came, or not seriously. But probably he would not have felt free to come, if Rose had not set him free. Quid pro quo . . . well, that is how *he* would see it.

Serious, brought down, he looked straight at her, to avoid accusations of evasion, and said, 'I would have to tell her. She would find out anyway. She would know.'

'Yes, she would.'

'But why not, Sarah? Why ever not? There must be limits to being a good . . . provider.'

What he had been going to say she didn't know. A good husband? A good father?

What she was thinking was: living with Rose has softened your brain. This is the kind of thing she goes in for, having your cake and eating it and pretending nothing has happened.

'Look, why don't we two go to Scotland? You remember all that, Sarah?'

They had been on a three weeks' walking tour in Scotland, just before they married in 1958.

'We could go next month,' he urged. 'I've got three weeks due.'

She shut her eyes, remembering the two of them walking up a heather-covered mountainside.

'Sarah,' she heard, gruff, accusing, 'I've been thinking about you so much. There's such a terrible gap in my life. There has been, for years.'

She said dryly, eyes still shut, 'Polygamy! You'd like that!' But she was smiling, she could not stop.

'Yes, yes,' he shouted, and reached her in two long strides. 'Yes, if that's what it is, *yes*.'

The little armchair by the fire had no companion, and he reached out a long arm and pulled across a chair in which he sat, close beside her. He put his arm around her.

'Sarah,' he crooned, his cheek on hers. 'Sarah,' he went on saying, while their cheeks glued themselves together with tears.

Suddenly the little room dazzled and glared. A sunbeam hitting a windowpane had been reflected onto a mirror just above their heads, and this in turn sent lozenges and prisms of colour onto a wall. Now it was like sitting in a pool of glittering water, submerged furniture, flowers, and themselves.

She freed herself from him, got up, pulled curtains across the end window. The curtains were white and unlined. That wall was now flat and white-shadowed, with a large rectangle where hot orange pricked through. Part of this rectangle lifted, and a tangerine-coloured sail swelled out into the room and subsided. In a few moments the sunlight would cease to beat against the back of the curtains, and the whole wall would be a dead flat white.

Their mood had quite changed.

She did not dare go and sit by him again. If she did, she would sink into . . . into . . .

He was gazing at her through the warm orange light that soaked everything.

'Sarah?' he inquired, as if searching for her in a maze.

He stood up, said, 'All the same, why not, Sarah? I don't see one good rational reason why not! I want you in my life! I need you! I simply cannot do without you.'

He came to her, bent, and gently rubbed his cheek against hers: it was a husband's, not a lover's, claim.

And then he was off, and she heard him bounding down the stairs.

*   *   *

The room was dimming. The glare behind the curtains no longer delineated every thread of the coarse linen. The shrill warning clatter of the birds in the plane tree was an evening sound, not the companionable gossiping of the day. The light abruptly faded off the curtains. That wall was now uninterruptedly white.

She sat down in the chair by the flowers. She looked at them critically. The jug was too smug, too contented a round shape for the gawky, stiff awkwardness of the cherry and the fresh spring lilac with its loose random flowers. She moved the jug to the floor behind her, and tried to think.

She was in a boil of emotions that were resolving into a single need: to escape . . . run away, in fact. Run, run, run out of this room, this building, out of London, yes, out of England. She was now out of her chair, and moving clumsily and fast about the room, like a shut-in bird. But what on earth was all this about? She had to run away from James, was that it? But this meeting of theirs had nothing of threat in it; on the contrary, for it had seemed as if some spell had been taken off them that until now had made every meeting, even a telephone call, an angry, guilty, embarrassed misery. Being with James today had been more like the first meeting of people who are going to love each other, full of recognitions and sweet surprises. But her heart was pounding, her stomach hurt, and she was being ravaged by anxiety.

She forced herself to sit down again, composing her limbs to suit her position, that of an elderly lady considering her situation with sober common sense. She was eyeing the telephone, she observed, as if her nerves expected it to ring, and unpleasantly.

If James had gone straight home, and if Rose was at home, then of course something about him would instantly have alerted her, even if he had not said at once – which was more likely – 'I've just been talking to Sarah, oh no, don't worry, I just dropped in on an impulse, that's all, nothing more to it.' She could positively hear him saying it.

Crisis could easily have taken over that house. Rose would already be on the telephone to her current confidante. She had one at a time, in an intense and dramatic bond, full of intimate meetings and vibrant conversations, but then there would be a quarrel, and another ex-intimate of whom she would say, 'I'm not going *there* if I'm likely to meet *her*, the cow!' She might at this very moment be saying to whoever it was, 'My God! Do you know what has happened? I'm losing my husband, that's all! He's started seeing his first wife – yes, Sarah! For God's sake, I've *got* to talk about it, it's urgent. No, cancel it! Come at once, please . . .'

While waiting for this tête-à-tête, which would be the first of very many, several a day, Rose would be laying out the cards, consulting *I Ching*, and making an appointment with her fortune-teller, a woman of limitless psychological penetration who was as familiar with her (Sarah's) life, as she was with Rose's; she (Sarah) had been pronounced of no threat to Rose; but her type, the Fair Lady, standing in opposition to Rose as Dark Lady, was, and always would be.

Rose lived in terror of some slim blonde nymphet. By the time the confidante arrived, Fate would already have pronounced through several mouths, or at least have given some pretty definite indications. As a result of the meeting between the two women all kinds of things would start to happen. The first, that her telephone (Sarah's) would start to ring. Someone she had never heard of would be saying, 'Do forgive me for bothering you, but I believe you can help me, actually James suggested it. Can you tell me something about Manchester? You were there, he said? You had a house there, didn't you? What are the schools like?'

Yes, James would know this call was going to be made, for Rose would have said in an airy, confident way, challenging James with a bold, laughing look, 'Oh, James, Sarah could advise, couldn't she? She knows all about Manchester!' All kinds of telephone calls and even happenings, none of them unreasonable, and on the face of it the essence of civilized good sense. Just like James coming to see her this afternoon. On the face of it . . .

Telephone calls from another of Rose's best friends – like a schoolgirl she only had best friends – 'Oh, Sarah, do you remember me, we met at the Tillings', do you remember? I hear you are going off with James to Wales? If you are going anywhere near Swansea, would you drop in and see an old friend of mine, she's so lonely these days since her husband died, she would be more than happy to put you both up, it would be such a kindness.'

Soon, a telephone call from Rose herself. The low, vibrant voice, always hinting at things that simply could not be said. 'Sarah, this is Rose! Yes, Rose! I've been wanting to really get to know you for such a long time . . . Do you think we could meet and have a real talk? No, I've discussed it all with James, and he'd love it. Would you invite me to tea? I'd love to see your flat, James says it's so pretty. Oh, I'd love to live in a flat, just by myself, just to be free, and *myself*, you understand?'

There would be many other telephone calls from Rose, casual, offhand, insulting. 'Sarah, is James there? No, but I thought . . . oh, I must have been mistaken. If he does drop in, do tell him to ring me, there's been a bit of a crisis, he's got to deal with it.'

While all this went on, Rose would be saying to absolutely everyone, 'I'm sorry to say there's a crisis in my marriage. James and I are both working at it, we have been so happy, and I'm sure it will all be right in the end.'

Her love affair would have been given up, after many weepy meetings. 'I have to make a choice, my darling love. Oh it isn't easy . . . the children . . .'

People would in fact be expecting the marriage to end. It was Rose's fourth. Her story, as far as it could be ascertained, for it changed with whomever she was telling it to, was something like this. She had emerged from the miseries of Europe after the war having already experienced everything in the way of hunger, of cold, and the threat of death. Her mother had died in a concentration camp, in some versions, but in others she had abandoned Rose for a lover. Rose, who was very pretty, married an American in the occupying force, whom she had madly loved, though some people knew, without condemning her, that she had become this man's mistress because if one wanted to eat, one had to attach oneself to one of the new armies.

Then she married another American, much better placed than the first. But she said she hated America, which was why she married an Englishman who was important in the oil empires of the world. He had adored her, this exotic, clever waif, but he did not adore her long. He was reputed to have said that he should have refused to marry her, and kept her as a mistress. She would never be a wife. It was like having a beautiful spoiled pet in the house, something like a cheetah, that couldn't be house-trained. That marriage had lasted three years.

Rose had done some serious thinking, and taken the advice of her fortune-teller. She was already well into her thirties. Married to James she had been a real wife, a good one, presiding over comfort and good meals, with one satisfactory baby after another. These were in themselves evidence of remarkable strength of mind, for everyone knew she had had 'dozens' of abortions and miscarriages. Each pregnancy, and then birth, had claimed the attention not only of James, midwives, doctors, hospitals, friends, neighbours, but circles of people who had scarcely heard of Rose, so remarkable and unprecedented did it turn out to be.

Sarah had contemplated these dramas with dislike, with distaste, and, above all, with incredulity that James could tolerate it all. One simply did not make a fuss about physical suffering (or any suffering if it came to that); one shut up, kept a stiff upper lip, bit the bullet, et cetera and so forth. Forced by Rose to examine these tenets, this *English* creed, Sarah concluded there was nothing wrong with it, and there was no virtue at all in all these foreign histrionics which, in Rose's case, were always compounded with dishonesty, with calculations so devious that sometimes it was years later before one understood what had really been going on.

Quite soon after inviting herself to tea, Rose was going to ring up and say something like this: 'Sarah! Yes, it's me, it's Rose! Sarah, I wonder if you would come to dinner? No, oh, don't say you won't without thinking about it. Why not, Sarah? We have so many friends in common, not to mention James, oh no, I don't mean that badly, I swear I don't, Sarah, oh, do believe me . . .'

She could see herself, one of several guests around that capacious family table, James at one end, Rose at the other, the children eyeing the adults as her own two had done her: polite, even deferential towards these appalling and cruel inevitabilities, but with nervous glances at each other, with wide, scared smiles. They would eat quickly and make excuses to leave the table and go to their rooms, where they would sit and discuss fearfully, angrily, but full of loud derision (because of their fear) the dangerous situation downstairs. 'Our father's first wife has come to supper . . . Sarah, oh don't you know about Sarah? Well, she's here for supper. Can I come over to your house?' So they would talk on the telephone to some friend.

Soon after this civilized and creditable-to-everyone family supper, James would say, with that resentful but admiring laugh he used to meet the situations Rose put him into, 'Sarah, Rose suggested we should take the two older children with us when we go off to France. They are very good at walking, you know. I took them to the Lake District last year. Would you mind?'

She would say she didn't mind. And probably she wouldn't. By then she would have become great friends with all the children, and a lot of her time would be taken up in choosing them presents and all the votive offerings children do need these days. She would have become – not a second mother, Rose would see to that – but a nice auntie, to all the children. She would say to James, 'How nice to have Sam and Betty along. What a pity the other two aren't old enough to come too, but perhaps next year. Of course I don't mind their coming. Why not?'

Except that her heart beat, her palms were itchy with sweat, and she was again prowling around the room as if preparing to leap through a window and into the street and be off – to anywhere at all.

What power that woman had! Always!

It was the strength of unscrupulousness, rooted in self-ishness, and born from – stupidity. It had never, ever, occurred to Rose that one should *not* do this or that. (But of course there was the question of that childhood in the camps. Did this mean that one would never, ever, judge Rose by ordinary standards?) During Sarah's bad time, when she had thought, much too much, about Rose, she had always come up against this, like running headlong into a glass barrier that stood between Rose and the rest of the world. To say to Rose, 'But one can't do that, don't you see?' To say, 'But that's not the decent thing to do!' – why, even in imagination when it is easy to see oneself saying this and that to an antagonist, the words simply would not get themselves formed.

But . . . stupidity? If it was that, then it got Rose everything. Sarah's husband. Four children. A large house. Stability after being flotsam. A man whose life was captive to her needs. Stupidity! No, it was a force, a power, that came from some level of human existence Sarah had never entered. When she had watched James go off to Rose, she had felt exactly as she would had she seen him, in a dream, pulled into a bewitched forest governed by primitive laws. She had felt he was leaving his own best self.

But then, there were the children. Over and over again during those years she had said to herself, 'Sarah, there are four children. Four children, Sarah. You can't argue with that.' Every child brings with it the unknown, brings possibilities and chances rooted in the distant past of humanity, possibilities stretching away into the future. James might have gone off into the enchanted forest after a witch, but there he had found four packages addressed to himself, each one full of Fate.

She supposed that Rose was James's *anima*, embodying a whole parcel of attributes that James's daylight self most deeply needed. She could see there was no fighting that.

It was Rose's fortune-teller who had said Rose was James's *anima*. And where had Sarah's comparable male been? Often enough Sarah had dwelled, but no more than adequately, on the two men with whom she had had affairs after James left her. Affairs are not easy, with adolescent children already sensitized to be on the watch for wrongdoing, not easy when you are holding down a job, and having to move to this or that town or country to keep it, always juggling children, their needs, term times, holidays, flats, houses, travelling. Her two affairs had been pleasant enough, if harassed and circumscribed by all these problems, and indeed the men in question put that rich relishing smile on her face whenever she thought of them. But she did not believe they represented any more than themselves.

No, it was James, she believed, who embodied that man who was her imperative, her other self. But there seemed to be an imbalance somewhere in the psychological equation. Often enough she had tried to picture some dark, dramatic, vibrant *lying* man who would silence all her best instincts, but she had concluded at last that this force could only be female. (She did not like this conclusion because she was a feminist.) She could not imagine a man with Rose's attributes. She had never met one, or even read about one. A man like Rose would be degenerate, or criminal.

But Rose was not degenerate or criminal. She was simply – female. Of a certain type that every woman at once and instinctively recognized at first sight. And every man had to respond to, at once, either with attraction, or unease and dislike. No man was ever indifferent to Rose.

Rose had only to walk into a room . . .

Ten years after she and James had married, ten happy years – and James always made a point of granting that, being fair, decent, and honourable – the two of them went to a party together. They had got there late because of some problem with a baby-sitter.

In the middle of a room stood a couple, a dark dramatic-looking woman, and a very young man. He was a boy, really, a poetic English boy, like Rupert Brooke. She was fascinating him. He was hypnotized by her. She was tall and slender, though this could hardly be discerned under swirling draperies, for she wore a gown made out of a scarlet, silver-broidered sari. Her black glistening hair snaked down her shoulders and back. One strand lay on a slim brown arm, and – this was Sarah's immediate, sardonic observation – this seductive coil was being kept there on sleek and shining skin by an angle of that arm, the elbow lifted, making a tender, poignant curve. Rose was not beautiful, but everyone was looking at her; and at the poor young man, kept helpless by the black depths of her eyes.

Sarah was indignant that the youth was being used in this way. Rose was sending out sly swift glances to the men who were watching, to judge her effect on them, and glances of connivance at the women who, and she would never ever understand this, were hating her for it, and would not send back equal glances. 'Look what a fool I am making of this poor male sucker,' was what she expected all the women present to share. Sarah looked at James, counting on him to feel what she felt, but she saw that his look at Rose was like the young man's. He was already lost with his first view of Rose, while his good wife Sarah was engaged at feeling ashamed for her sex at its worst. What Sarah was thinking at the very moment her husband was losing his senses, his good sense, was, 'She's *female*, she's female in a basic gutter way that every decent woman in the world hates.'

He walked straight over to Rose. People looked at Sarah standing there, abandoned, for she had been: nothing could have been more blatant. The poor poetic youth, forgotten from that moment, stumbled to one side as James took his place. And that was how Sarah had lost her husband to Rose, as simply and as inevitably as that. When the time came to go home, she touched him on the arm, and he came away from Rose with whom he had been talking for three hours, not looking at his wife or at anyone else.

She took the bemused man home, and he came to the

same bed, and he lay awake, and so did she, listening to how he sighed and suffered, and there was a moment towards morning, the early light already in the room, when he said, 'But Sarah, what happened? I don't understand. Did I behave badly?'

Everyone in that room knew what had happened. That very next morning Olive, the couple's great friend, rang up Sarah and said, 'Forget it, there's nothing you can do, it'll have to run its course.'

And 'it' was still running its course.

'It' was about to engulf her too.

'Sarah,' said Sarah to herself, as elderly people do. 'Sarah, do you realize you are thinking of actually running away? Running out of this flat, which you like, from this city, which you love, simply to get away from Rose, get away from . . . ?

'No, come on, surely you are exaggerating. Suppose you do exactly what James suggests, neither more nor less. You will go off with him for three weeks on a walking trip (and what you are imagining now is the delight, not of lovemaking, but of talking, talking with someone who perfectly understands you, your other self), and it doesn't matter where you go – Scotland, Timbuktu. You will of course insist that Rose should be told, for that is the decent and honourable thing to do. You will *not* respond to her telephone calls, but simply be polite, no more, nor to the indirect telephone calls, each one of which will have the unmistakable flavour of Rose's deviousness. You will not become a guest at Rose's table, or a kind auntie to her children – part, in short, of Rose's life, her family, that *quicksand*. You will simply go off with James for a walking holiday and that is that! All simple and aboveboard.'

Sarah sank down in her little straightbacked armchair and closed her eyes. She was being absurd. Even to begin to think like this meant she was already sucked in.

'No,' she would have to tell James. 'No, no, no, James, it simply will not do, you must see that.' He would have seen it at once, if he had not spent fifteen years with Rose.

Even before the telephone rang she was staring at it as if it was about to explode.

Cautiously she lifted the handpiece and said, 'Yes?'

A child's voice.

'Is that Sarah?' said a little girl (Betty, probably, in a breathless voice that had in it, already, all of Rose's shamelessness).

'Yes,' said Sarah.

'Is my father there?'

'No,' said Sarah.

Prompted by Rose, the child said, 'Thank you,' and the line went dead.

Sarah was standing by the telephone in a dark room, and the two tall side windows showed tenebrous branches against a hazy sky. She was weakened already. She was unable to prevent thoughts of what it would be like with James back in her life. Good Lord, how much he had taken with him, when he left her for Rose! And now, how easy not to go away (*run* away, she was fiercely accusing herself); how easy to stay and see it through to the end.

The end? Why the *end*?

Sarah switched on the lights, and stood in a small bright room, the night shut away from her. She was breathing fast, her whole being prickling with some kind of energy ... it was hard to keep still, she was striding around that room of hers, so much too small for her. She saw in one of the little mirrors a distressed, wild-looking creature with distracted eyes, and with moving lips, too. She was muttering to herself, this woman, this Sarah – herself.

She was muttering, 'It's not me, it's her. Not Sarah, Rose.'

What did she mean by that ... 'What *is* it?' she demanded of herself irritably. 'What is the matter?' For she felt as if she was being invaded by some understanding that was like a powerful substance, changing her. 'Rose, it's Rose. Not me, but Rose.' These words were on her lips forcing her to attend to them.

She switched off the lights again and stood by the window in the end wall. The disorder of the gardens was hidden by the dark, and all she could see were roofs against the sky.

She shut her eyes. She breathed slowly. She was seeing (the picture forced itself on her, the fragile arms of a young girl stretching upward out of some kind of pit, or trap. Golden brown arms, with a fine sheen of dark hair ... the child's fingers reached up, closed on the edge of the pit, and then big boots came crunching down, and the arms fell back but crept up again, and tenacious fingers clutched at the loose soil that crumbled as she tried to hold it. The delicate arms tensed there, trembling ...). Sarah shut her eyes so as not to see the big boots come stamping down.

How had pretty young girls got themselves out of all that ... how had they survived?

Sarah was a child in the war, and while it went on her view of it was the conventional one presented to her by the necessities of wartime. Her father was in the Air Force. After the war both parents were involved with helping refugees out of the shambles that was Europe. Sarah had known about 'all that'. But without knowing about it. Still a child she had told herself, 'Of course one can't really understand what it is like, all that, not if one is English.' Meaning, 'not if you've been safe all your life.' (And will go on being safe, was implicit.) 'All that' was a horror outside ordinary living, and there was no point dwelling on it, because if one hadn't been in it, one would never understand. Sarah had closed a door in herself. Rather, she had refused to open it. And yes, she believed she was right to do it. One needn't allow oneself to wallow in horrors.

When she had first heard Rose's history she had listened and kept the door shut. For one thing she did not believe it. Yes, she knew Rose had been there, had escaped from 'all that'. Not necessarily, however, in the way she said. Rose was a liar. She lied as she breathed. Rose was one of those people who, if they say they walked up a street on the right side going east, one automatically corrected it to 'the left side, going west'.

Rose had been – so she had told some people – in a concentration camp. Had told others, more than one. Her mother had died in a camp. Her father was a fabulously rich South American who had had this amazing love affair with her beautiful mother, but he was married and had gone back to his wife. True? Who knew! (Who cared, Sarah had added, in moments of moral exhaustion. There was always too much of Rose!)

Sarah knew that a lot of people who had emerged from 'all that' said they were in camps, and perhaps they had been, but the words stood for a horror that people who had not been part of 'all that' did not have to enter. Could not enter. A kind of shorthand, that's what these words were . . . the camps had only been part of it. They were a black pit into which people were sucked, or thrown, or fell, but around it people had struggled and fought to save themselves, save others, in ways that no outsider could imagine. Rose had emerged from 'all that', and if her stories weren't true, what of it?

She had come out. She had survived. That was enough.

She had three times been the petted, petulant, child-wife, mistress-wife, of adoring men who had got rid of her because she could not fit herself into being ordinary, being a wife.

How had she seen that? She had played a part she had to believe in, because it brought her out of the black pit, because it had saved her, but then it hadn't been appropriate after all. She had then decided to become a good wife, all home-made bread and noisy children in a family house. But she had had to make the decision to be that. This Rose, the good wife of James, was a construct, a role, just as the other, the petted, pretty, child-mistress had been.

Rose had never understood this world, the safe, ordered world, which was not 'all that'. She had never ever been able to grasp the rules that governed it. Yes, they were mostly unwritten rules, and yes of course one absorbed them as one grew up, the way Sarah had.

Rose had not.

Sarah stood by the window in a dark room with her eyes shut, and her perspectives had so far changed that she was almost Rose, she was feeling with her. And what she felt (Sarah now knew, in her own bones and flesh) was panic. Fear was the air Rose breathed. She was like someone continually reaching out for hand-holds that seemed solid but gave way. Three husbands, married for safety, had crumbled in her hands, leaving her desperate, determined to find – James.

And now James, this marriage, was giving way.

This love affair (with another poetic young Englishman, so Sarah had heard) was another face of panic – middle-aged Rose was trying to reassure herself that she could still attract.

Sarah began replaying in her mind the scenes she foretold earlier.

Rose, frantic, desperate, distraught with fear, on the telephone to a 'best friend', who she had to know by now would suddenly cease to be a friend, because Rose was too much, because of her excessiveness. 'I have too much vitality, too much energy for the English!' she would complain, while those great black eyes of hers looked inward, full of incomprehension, wondering what she had done *this* time. You have been lying again, Sarah told Rose's image. But Rose would never understand what Sarah meant. Rose lied as she breathed about absolutely everything, but for her this was just survival, it was what had saved her, had got her out of the horrible place that was her childhood. Rose wove nets around James, that he would never understand, just as she could never understand him.

Rose would never, ever, understand ordinary decency, common sense, honesty. One did not learn these qualities when part of 'all that'.

Weaving nets and snares, crazy with fear, using every trick she knew, she would pull her rival Sarah towards her, into that house, that family, and then . . . The great family table with the children around it, and their friends. James at the head of the table, and sometimes his colleagues. She, Rose, at its foot. Olive . . . other people . . . And there, too, Sarah, sitting modestly in her place at the side of the table, with the children, like a visitor. Her husband (Rose's) with his first wife, the two Northerners, two elderly Vikings, handsome if sun- and wind-dried, humorous, judicious, not commenting on this scene, and not even allowing their eyes to meet (which in itself would be enough to drive Rose hysterical with suspicion for she always and with everyone used those great eyes of hers in glances, connivings, little raisings of the brow, dark meaningful looks – she could not manage without them! Had never managed without them, her atmosphere of me-and-you)

... but there they sat, her husband and Sarah, calm, smiling, undramatic, and at home in a world that Rose did not understand, and could not, for she had been born into that other place, where people survived.

Rose could do not other than weave nets around Sarah, using James to do it. She would plot and plan and intrigue, lay snares for the world she could not understand, and she would pull it into her life and into her home and sit it at her table.

And then?

And then she would kill herself. There was nothing else for her. Her panic, her horror, would not be assuaged, appeased, because Sarah, obedient, amenable, sat at her table, but, on the contrary, it would rise up in her and kill her.

Of course!

It was obvious!

It had been obvious from the start, and that was why Sarah had been in such a panic herself. To get out . . . to get away . . . to make sure none of these things would happen.

'Rose, not Sarah.' 'Her, not me,' she had heard herself muttering, from that part of her (that part of us all) which was so much more intelligent than the slow, lumbering, daylike self.

Rose would ring herself, tonight. Or another of the children would. Or James would, with a message from Rose.

Sarah would simply not answer the telephone.

Meanwhile she switched on the lights, found a certain letter in a drawer, and dialled her old friend Greta in Norway. 'Greta,' she said firmly. 'I want to accept your invitation, but I have a great favour to ask. I want to come now, at once. I want to come and use you as a base for walking trips, yes, all summer, a long time . . . And I don't want anyone to know where I am. I don't want James to know. Or Rose. Not anyone. All right? Yes, I'll ring you from Oslo.'

There, it was done.

She briskly began to collect the clothes she would need.

Tomorrow she would put her home into the hands of an estate agent, and go at once to the airport.

Tonight, now, she would go out to dinner at a restaurant, not come home until late, and she would not answer the telephone . . . which was ringing as she ran down the stairs away from it.

Two Old Women and a Young One

The restaurant is used by publishers, by agents, and – if guests of one or the other – by authors. About the restaurant nothing much can be said: it is yet to be explained why one restaurant is more popular than another whose food is also adequate. It was perhaps too interestingly decorated, but at the same time it aspired to opulence. It is always full.

Midday. People were arriving for lunch. By themselves at a favoured table beside a cascade of cream-and-green ivies were two old women. They were smartly dressed but fussily, with scarves, necklaces, earrings. Actresses? Was there a suggestion of self-parody in those eyelashes, the eye paint?

They sat catercornered. Their table was set for a third. They refused an aperitif, then, as the restaurant went on filling, they asked for sherries.

'Very dry,' said one, to the waiter, and the voice announced that she was older than she seemed, for it wavered.

'Very dry,' said the other, a good octave lower, in a voice once pitched to be sexy, but now it rumbled on the edge of a croak.

'Very good,' said the waiter, and he lingered a moment, smiling. He was a lively young Frenchman.

'Perhaps we have the wrong day?' remarked one.

'I am sure we have not,' said the other.

And here came their host, a youngish man almost running to them, blank-eyed with anxiety. 'I'm so sorry,' he as good as wept, and ran his hand back over his boyish hair, disordered as it was by apology and by haste. He sat and the same waiter nodded, as he called, 'Champagne, the usual.'

'Dear me,' said one old woman, 'we are being spoiled.' She was, perhaps, the prettier, a delightful old thing. Younger she must have been delightful, a rose, blue-eyed, blonde, and her hair even now was silver, a mass of intricate waves, tendrils, not unlike the casque favoured by old Queen Mary.

'Indeed we are,' said the other in her deep voice. She had certainly been striking, with dark eyes and, probably, hair. Now it was gold, a pale gold, in a modified chignon, held with a black velvet bow.

Sisters?

'I was held up on your account – not that it's an excuse,' said the host, and reached for the just-filled champagne glass. He waited only long enough for politeness, for as the other two glasses began to bubble and bead he swallowed down his first glass and at once the waiter refilled it. The two women watched and exchanged the briefest glance.

'It's all sorted out,' said the publisher. 'There will be two contracts, both on the same terms. It is being assumed you two will contribute equally to the book.'

'Oh, good,' said silver-hair. 'Well, that's agreed, then. I'm so glad.' And she put back her champagne, in a gulp, and smiled gently at him.

'Of course,' said gold-head, in her throaty voice. 'I was sure you'd sort it all out.' And she, too, drank off her glass.

'How nice,' said silver-hair, 'to drink champagne at lunchtime.' Her voice was already more quavery than it had been, and when it reached for lower notes it achieved a reminiscent intimacy.

'How nice,' said gold-head, 'to drink champagne with a handsome young man.'

'Oh come on,' said he, bluffly, startled. Quite upset he was. William was his name: call-me-William, but he wouldn't say this to these two who, it was obvious, would take advantage in some way.

The two women were focusing on him an inspection that he experienced as an intrusion. He was saying to himself, in a moment of panic, that between them they claimed almost a century and a half of years.

He sat staring over his champagne glass at the two old women. He had not met them before, only spoken on the telephone, and as a result of these talks he had personally overlooked every clause of the contracts. He had not expected . . . well, he was shocked. Nothing in his experience had taught him how to see these two worldly old trouts, now both tight on a couple of swallows of champagne.

'Darling,' said silver-hair, 'we've scared him.' And she put her hand, shapely but blotched with age and full of rings, on his forearm.

'Don't mind us,' said gold-head, it seemed to him with a quite grotesque naughtiness, 'but it is all going to our poor heads.'

Meanwhile the waiter was observing all this. He filled the three glasses.

'We both of us live alone, you see,' said silver-hair, explaining it all to him.

'Oh, I thought you lived together . . . I don't know why I did . . .'

'We may be sisters, but we haven't come to that yet.'

'We're still hoping for something better, you see,' said gold-head, and then gave a snort of derisive laughter, God knows at what.

'Living alone with my baby,' said silver-hair, who in fact was Fanny Winterhome.

'And I live with mine, and we both love our babies,' said gold-head, Kate Bisley.

They were widows. They had been theatrical agents for thirty years, had known 'everybody', had represented a thousand good troupers, famous and less famous, and now they were writing their reminiscences. The book would certainly sell for its anecdotes about the great, pretty near the bone some of them. 'But never spiteful, darling, we promise you,' Fanny had assured him on the telephone. There was also the question of their theatre expertise, past and present. No one knew more than they did, he had been assured.

Yesterday the young (youngish) publisher had been told, quite by chance, by a well-known actor he had asked to help 'promote' the book, that the two women had been beautiful.

He sat looking from one to the other.

'Kate has a Burmese, and my baby is a Siamese,' said Fanny. And her rouged lips kiss-kissed the air, an invisible pussycat.

'I think we had better order,' he said firmly.

It was evident he cared about what he ate, and they did not. But as the waiter approached to drain the end of the champagne into the three glasses the host said, hypnotized into doing it – he was convinced – 'Another bottle, I think.'

'Oh good,' sighed Fanny. 'One can never have too much champagne.'

'One can at this time of the day,' said Kate.

'Well, we'll have to support each other to the train.'

'Or perhaps this handsome man would escort us there?'

'I certainly would, with pleasure, but I have an appointment I simply cannot be late for.'

'Oh dear, then we mustn't expect too much of you,' Fanny said, patting the pretty silver lattice above her pearl-bubbled left ear while her rings flashed. A ring caught in the hair. 'Oh damn,' she said, 'I've got out of the way of dolling myself up.' And she unclipped the earring, laid it on the cloth, unclipped the other, took off a ring or two.

'It was all for you,' said Kate, 'but we are out of practice, you see.' She was offering herself to him in the tones of her deep voice, just as Fanny did her light one. Their voices . . . while he smiled and tucked heartily into his starter, prawns and bits of this and that, he was trying to come to terms with their voices.

'Aren't you even going to ask about the terms?' he enquired, whimsically, but with an undernote of grudge.

'Oh I'm sure you've done well by us,' said Fanny, her voice tinkling down his spine.

'Besides, you wrote us the terms, have you forgotten?' said Kate, and her deep bell made a descant with Fanny's chime.

Damn them, he was thinking.

'Besides, it's not likely you would try to cheat us,' said Fanny, 'when we were the best agents in the business in our time.'

'True,' he said.

Both, having allowed the tines of their forks to dawdle in their fish, put down the forks and reached as one woman for their glasses.

'Bliss,' said Fanny, sipping.

'Bliss plus,' echoed Kate.

He was looking past them at a table visible through a slight arch, where sat a young woman, who was facing

him. She was entertaining an influential New York publisher, and was not looking at him, though she must
have seen him there. She was more attractive, in style
not unlike the Modigliani we all know so well. She had
a long voluptuous white throat. Her black hair glistened
like clean coal, and was cut in what was once called a bob.
She had green eyes, and wore a grass-green jumper with
a string of jet beads. Her skin was white, with the thick
glistening look of camellia petals. He certainly was not
the only man looking at her. But she had eyes only for
the man opposite her, attending to him like .·.. well, like
a mistress determined to please. He acknowledged that it
would not have occurred to him to make this comparison
if he had not been subjected to these two old . . .

As she continued not to acknowledge him, he leaned
back again, prepared to put up with being embarrassed.

They had noticed his absence of mind, and sat as quiet
as two pampered budgies, drinking, musing, it seemed,
about long-ago things – attractive memories, for their
wrinkled mouths smiled, and their eyes were damp with
champagne.

He began on his main course, while they patiently,
but indifferently, waited for him. They had said they
didn't want a main course. Urged again now to change
their minds, Fanny said, 'The pudding! That's what I'm
waiting for. I adore, adore sweet things now. I never
used to.'

'Sweets to the sweet,' said Kate, apparently compliment-
ing Fanny for him, since it didn't occur to him to do so. Or
was this a moment from her own past?

Both were now quite tipsy, and Kate actually swayed
a little, and unsteadily hummed a bar or two of – what?

Fanny put her head on one side, lips pursed, and Kate
said triumphantly, 'I've Got You Under My Skin.'

'What a tune to dance to, that was,' said Fanny. 'Do

you dance?' she enquired, caressing him with her old sweet voice.

'No, they don't dance these days,' said Kate. 'We danced. They none of them do. Not real dancing. They just jump about.'

'No,' he confessed, fortifying himself with champagne. 'I don't actually ever seem to . . .'

The second bottle was almost gone. No, he simply would not, he was damned if he would, order a third.

He had swallowed down his food, and had not enjoyed it.

He nodded, and knew it was desperate, at the waiter, who, it was obvious, knew exactly how to deal with these *monstres sacrées*. He came gracefully forward, smiling, bestowing his attention on both, in friendly glances, and began detailed explanations of the desserts. He might have been describing jewels, or orchids. His manner was full of flattery, and of appreciation, of the food, and certainly, of them. He had a favourite granny perhaps? The three were positively flirting! It was quite charming, as a performance, the host was prepared to concede that. When it was finally agreed that a certain confection of chocolate and *crème fraîche* was what they had to eat, the waiter pointed out it was not wise to let all those pretty things – for both women had now made piles of jewellery beside them – lie about anyhow on the tablecloth. He smiled, they smiled, and both swept up their valuables and let them fall into their handbags.

'How do you know I wouldn't run off with them myself?' enquired the waiter laughing, departing to fetch their desserts.

'Oh don't be silly,' sighed Kate after him.

'He's a dish,' said Fanny. 'I'm sure there are more good-looking young men about than there used to be.'

'An illusion,' said Kate.

They seemed to have forgotten him, or had given him up, for they sat meditating and not looking anywhere near him.

They ate their confections in lingering, appreciative licks and sips, but no, this performance was not meant for him, the host, who sat watching, trying to see them as the waiter clearly did, charming women, for when he had an unoccupied moment, he stood nearby, smilingly watching.

Last week a certain impresario had remarked that these two had been the dishiest women in London.

Dishy. A dish. Dishes. Dishiest.

The champagne was quite gone.

No, neither drank coffee these days and brandy would be too much of a good thing. They were quite happy to toddle off to their train.

He told the waiter he would be back to pay the bill, and he took them out, one on either arm. This contact disturbed him, but he did not propose to analyse why. The waiter was holding the door open, 'Au revoir, au revoir,' he said. 'Come back, madame, do come back, madame.'

And, before turning back to his duties, he stood looking after them, and gave the minutest shrug, regretful, philosophic, humorously tender.

There was a taxi almost at once. The host handed them in, both slightly unsteady, but in command of themselves. As he bent to smile goodbye, it occurred to him they were actually saying to themselves, and would to each other the moment he had turned away, 'Right, we've got that over.' A performance was done with. The very second their little waves at him – which seemed to him perfunctory, to say the least – were done with, they sat back and forgot him.

He returned to the restaurant. Now the Modigliani

girl was alone. He sat himself down at her table, just as another colleague did. The three of them worked in different departments of the same publishing firm.

'God,' said she, 'what one has to do for duty.' She smiled matily at first one and then the other, but holding their eyes with hers. An Armagnac stood before her. She was a little tight too. 'Drinking at lunchtime,' she complained.

At the next table sat a woman they all knew, an American agent in London. She greeted them, they greeted her, and she began to talk about her trip, enquiring about new young writers. Her voice resonated, commanded attention, as American professional women's voices often do, insistent, not conceding an inch, every syllable a claim.

The Modigliani girl answered her, and her voice was just as much in a local pattern as the American's. Somewhere in England, at a girls' school, at some time probably in the late sixties or early seventies, there must have been a headmistress, or even a head girl, of extreme force of character, or elegant, or rich, or pretty, but at least with some quality that enabled her to impose her style on everyone, making her enviable, copiable ... by a class – then a school – then by several. For often and everywhere is to be found this voice among professional women formed at that time. It is a little breathy high voice that comes from a circumscribed part of the women who use it, not more than two square inches of the upper chest, certainly not a chest cavity or resonating around a head. Oh dear, poor little me, they lisp their appeals to the unkind world; these tough, often ruthless young women who use every bit of advantage they can. Sometimes in a restaurant this voice can be heard from more than one of the tables; or from different parts of a room at a board meeting, or a conference. There they sat, in professional and competent discussion, the American tough guy, the English cutie, or sweetie, or dish, or dolly-face, perfect specimens of their kind, one insisting and grinding, one chitter-chattering, and smiling, turning her beautiful long white neck, curved and taut, while the black silky hair swung on her cheeks.

Two men watched and listened.

Then their girl, their colleague, turned her attention back to them. 'I'm going to play hookey this afternoon. I'm not coming back to my office,' she almost whispered, and her great emerald eyes widened like a little girl's at the dark. 'I want to get home and feed my baby. I've got myself a new friend, he's a baby chow, he's a little love . . .'

The waiter brought the old women's host his bill: he checked and signed.

Brought the beauty her bill: she signed having given it a fast cold inspection a million miles from this whispering confiding style, but reminded her colleagues of the sharpness she used in her work. Meanwhile she lisped, 'My life has changed. When Bill and I parted . . .' Bill was her recently divorced husband . . . 'I thought that was really it, you know, for ever, absolutely the *end* for me, but now I have my baby-love, I've lost my heart again. He sleeps on my bed, I try to keep him off, I've made him a little little nest on the floor – he's only the size of a big teddy, you know, but he won't have it . . .' She smiled at them, breaking their hearts.

All three should be back in the office, should have left here half an hour ago, should at least be leaving now, but she held them there: 'I take him out, I take my baby to the park every morning before I come to work, yes, it's a discipline, just like a real baby, and when I take him home I give him some little things to play with while I'm gone, he loves to play with green leaves or a twig. Oh he's so pretty, dancing about in the grass, he's like a baby lion . . .'

They sat on, and would until she broke it, got up to go, abandoned them.

But if they could not get up and leave her, then it seemed she could not end the business of charming them . . .

The Real Thing

The first time it was Jody who rang Sebastian, and the conversation went like this. 'Sebastian? Is that Sebastian? I am Jody. *Jody!* Don't you know who I am?'

A pause. 'Yes, I think so. You're Henry's new . . .'

'Hardly new, surely?'

A pause. 'Ah.' A pause.

'When did you hear about me?'

'Well . . . I've only just heard, actually.'

The effect was of an explosion at the other end of the line, but a silent one. 'You've only just heard about me? But . . . For Christ's sake I've been with Henry for over two years now.'

'I have to say that surprises me.'

'Does it? Nobody told you? Angela didn't say?'

A pause. 'No . . . look here . . . I'm not . . . I don't feel . . . I'm sorry . . .'

'Don't get all English with me, that's all I need.'

'What do you want?'

'That's better.' The voice was American – naturally, since that was what she was – loud, insistent, and tears or laughter were latent in it. 'I just wanted to talk, that's all. *Don't hang up on me.*'

'I hadn't intended to.'

'I am going to marry Henry, and you are going to marry Angela. The way I see it, stupid of me, I'm sure, that's enough of a bond for a short chat.'

'Look,' he began again, allowing it to be heard that his affability was at risk, 'I'm perfectly willing to talk about anything you like, but you come as a bit of a surprise.'

'You say Angela has never mentioned me?'

'No, nor Henry.'

'Henry! You mean, you see Henry?'

'Well, yes, sometimes. Civilized you know – all that.'

'Don't mention that word civilized to me,' she said violently. 'I'm sorry, but that word is *out*.'

'Very well. As you like. But yes, as it happens, Henry and I have met, you know, to discuss this and that.'

'But never me.'

'No, as it happens.'

'Good God, no, it's simply not . . . I just can't believe it, that's all.'

He said apologetically, 'You see, the subject never arose.'

'Oh, why should it! I'm only the woman who is going to marry Henry, that's all.'

A silence. 'But . . . Jody . . . Jody?'

'Jody. A name. Like Mary.'

'Or like Sebastian,' he said, with a small placatory laugh. 'Look, Jody, don't you see? We don't discuss – that sort of thing. I'm sure you don't discuss me with Henry? You've better things to talk about!'

'No, but then you're quite a new phenomenon, aren't you? You've just happened?'

'Hardly, I've known Angela about three years now – more.'

'Three years,' she said, intending to sound stunned.

'Something like that, yes. Henry hasn't mentioned me to you at all?'

'Angela's new *bloke*, he said.'

'Well! Oh well, and what of it? That's hardly the point, surely? I don't spend my time with Angela with the aim of discussing her ex-husband's love life.'

'I must tell you that if I'd known you were *there* I'd have rung you up long ago.'

'A pleasure,' said he.

'Oh no,' she said. 'Oh no no *no* . . . not that tone. Not that English *tone*. When I hear it I . . .'

'You reach for your revolver?'

'If I had one, yes. I'm not going to be switched *off*.'

Sudden anger, the anger of a man who expects too much of himself in the way of sweet reason. 'This is all too much of a good thing,' he exploded. 'If you want to talk, then talk, but I'm not sitting here as a substitute target for – someone or other.'

'Oh God,' she suddenly wailed. 'I'm sorry, oh I'm sorry, I didn't mean . . . I wanted to talk to you, I *had* to, I've simply got to find out . . . no, you're right. Sorry. Goodbye, Sebastian.'

He was alone. It was eleven at night, and he was ready for bed. Instead he poured himself a Scotch, not his custom at that hour, and sat looking at a dead television set, as if it might suddenly grant information. He was much more disturbed than he felt he ought to be.

A few months later it was he who rang her.

'Jody? Sebastian.'

'Hi, Sebastian,' she said, deliberately offhand, he was sure.

'I hope you don't mind,' he said cautiously, 'but I remembered you rang me once.'

'So I did.'

'Well, it's like this. Henry asked me to ring you to say he has gone off with Angela to see Connie in her school play. He tried to get you and couldn't, and he can't see you this weekend.' A silence. 'You see, he had forgotten about the play. Connie, you know – the child.'

A cautious stifled voice, which seemed to be trying out each word, listening to it. 'You mean, Henry, *my* loved one, asked *you*, his ex-wife's loved one, to ring *me* about *him* not seeing *me*?'

'That's about it, yes.'

A sound that could have been a sob, a curse, a prayer.

'Well,' said he. 'There you are.'

'Excuse me, but how do you come to be in a position to be passing on messages from Henry?'

'I was with Henry and Angela last night, as it happened.'

'A threesome?'

'No, actually a foursome. My wife – well, my former wife, was there too. Olga.'

'Listen,' she said, in a voice kept muted with an effort, 'I think that's all shit. I'm sorry.'

'I'm sorry, too. But what is?'

'Henry tells me I am a barbarian. That's what he says. I don't go for all this sweetness and light. It's not natural. It's not healthy. And it's *stupid*. There's nothing but pain in it for everyone.'

'A point of view, I suppose.'

'Oh *God*, if you only knew how I hate this humorous sterilizing of everything.'

'Everything *real*?'

'You said it. Right. Exactly so. Everything real.'

'And you don't believe people should be friendly after a divorce?'

'Once my divorce was through I said I never wanted to see him again. And I haven't. My ex-husband. Marcus.'

'Ah.'

'A louse.'

'But I thought you had a child together?'

'We do.'

'But you never meet.'

'No.'

'Ah.'

'Ah to you too. Well, message delivered, and thank you.' She rang off.

He attempted a laugh but again found himself pouring a drink.

Some months later she rang him. 'What's all this about you and I going up for a nice weekend at Henry and Angela's cottage?'

'It was mentioned.'

'And what did you say, Sebastian?'

'I said I thought it was premature.'

'Premature,' she screamed. 'Look, no, just a minute . . . I want us to meet. Just you and me. I want to talk.'

'What about?'

She laughed. He felt encouraged: that was a real laugh. That's better, he was thinking.

'What I want to talk about isn't – practicalities. Not where to put the children or who pays for what. There's something . . . I don't know exactly how to put it.' He did not say anything to encourage her, so there was a pretty long pause. Then she inquired, reasonably, 'Don't you ever feel as if you are up against something – well, intangible?'

'What sort of thing?'

'With those two. Henry and Angela.' He still did not help her, and she went on with difficulty. 'I mean, inadequate, that's what I feel, I don't match up.'

'Oh *that*,' said he, given a handhold. 'Of course, inadequate, but then, who doesn't feel inadequate?'

'For Christ's sake *no*, just don't do that.'

'What?'

'Just dismiss it.'

'I didn't know I had.'

'Of course you didn't. You people never do, do you?'

'Meaning us, the English?'

'Yes. That's it. Precisely.'

'But I understand you married one?'

'I did. And I am pledged to wed another, Henry. Marcus, then Henry. A rich education in sweeping things under the carpet.'

'It sounds to me as if we're not really your cup of tea.'

She laughed. 'Have you got anything against our meeting? A little chat? A meal?'

'You live in Manchester?'

'Yes, but I'm in London this weekend.'

'Do you want to come here?'

'Neutral ground. A restaurant.'

'Good God, I never thought of myself as a minefield. Or something.'

'Or something. What kind of restaurant?'

'I don't give a damn.'

'You don't? I'm told – far too often – that Angela is a perfect cook.'

'You can have too much of a good thing.'

'Oh. All right then, where?'

They agreed to arrive late at the restaurant, so as not to be hurried, and in fact the place was emptying. They sat examining each other with a curiosity due almost entirely to the absent Henry, the absent Angela. She was thinking, why should Angela get rid of one, and take on another just the same?

But he was thinking, My God, Henry's going to find her a handful, after Angela. And congratulated himself on getting the better bargain.

He was a tall, dark, rather stooped man – as if even the height he had seemed to him too obtrusive, and he was trying to lessen it. He wore conventionally good clothes.

He had a quizzical look, a sign, she was convinced, of the deprecatory humour that drove her wild. He was smiling politely at a dramatic blonde dressed – he felt strongly – much too handsomely for the occasion.

He was more on guard than he knew, although he had said to himself before arriving, Now, careful, the slightest thing sets her off. Every line of him said, 'Don't come too close.' He leaned back in his chair, even tilting it as she leaned forward towards him. She was aware that they must look as if she pursued him, but she did not care.

He was thinking that her voice did nothing for her. A pity, too, that Americans had to – as they would put – verbalize everything. Intelligent: she was evidently that. But a pity that . . .

Having got the ordering of the food out of the way – unimportant for this occasion, she said, 'Sebastian, how long have you been with Angela?'

He had to think. 'Four years. At least.'

'And I have been with Henry for three.'

'I hope you have enjoyed yourself as much as I have.'

This, which he had hoped would set the tone for their conversation, made her smile, wryly. Then he smiled too.

'All right,' said he, 'I'm doubtless an insensitive clod.'

'It has never bothered you that it took them so long to divorce? It was a perfectly simple divorce.'

'No, why should it?'

'Only a formality!'

'Do you see it as much more?'

'Yes, I do. I didn't at first, but then I began to wonder why nothing ever got started.'

'It's finished now, though. The thing was finally through last month.'

'But let's not be too precipitous, let's not be premature!'

He acknowledged that she teased with the briefest of smiles. Let's get on with it! – he was signalling.

'I feel all the time as if things are not being said, there's something I'm not getting to grips with.'

'So you said on the telephone.' Lest she take this as a put-off, he made a gesture which said, No, wait . . . He took a couple of therapeutic mouthfuls of wine, and his serious glance was meant to show he had every intention of meeting her honestly. But in spite of this he looked embarrassed and reluctant. 'I've been thinking about what you've been saying. You see, I don't think that I expect as much as you seem to. Of course there are barriers and difficulties. Henry and Angela were married for – I think it was ten years. They have a child – you know, Connie. All that isn't just going to disappear because of – well, you and me? And I have an ex-wife. Olga. Did I tell you? I expect Angela finds things not too easy with me sometimes. And you have an ex-husband – surely Henry must sometimes . . .'

'No,' she cut in decisively. 'No, absolutely not. I've cut that off. That's the point. Finished! *Finita! Basta!* I don't like ghosts in the machine.'

He sighed. He had not meant to, and now he looked guilty, and because of that she had to smile at him. Evidently Henry earned this smile often enough. A well-practised smile, he was thinking. 'Why do you expect so much?' he inquired. And this was the first (as she saw it) real thing he had said. He was speaking out of his own nature, and not what he believed he had to say out of self-defence. 'Perhaps I am not so difficult to please as you? I've had a perfectly splendid time with Angela these four years. And I hope to have many more.'

'I didn't say I hadn't had a perfectly splendid time with Henry,' she said sweetly. And they laughed. Together. They even liked each other, as much as was possible with those two invisible presences at the meal, Angela and Henry. 'But I don't see the point of marrying unless it's all there, you know, *everything*.'

'Ah well, then I think you're being unreasonable. Asking for trouble.'

'Why bother to get married?'

'Perhaps you shouldn't? No, I mean that – kindly, believe me. It's no good asking too much. It was the mistake I made with Olga.'

'Did you ever regret divorcing her? Olga?'

Now, a hesitation. He did not like this. 'Yes,' he said, with difficulty. 'Yes, I sometimes do. But we are the best of good friends.'

'Like Henry and Angela.'

'I hope so.'

'And like you and Henry.'

'I like Henry. My life is much better for Henry. He's one of the people I'd go to if I were in real trouble.'

'Rare.'

'I think so, yes.'

'Immature,' she sighed, histrionically. 'That's me. I haven't grown up.' And then, in one of the sudden, almost savage turns he had been dreading, 'Except that that is bullshit. Rubbish. Oh I know what you think of me. I've had it for years from Marcus, and now with Henry.'

'Marcus the louse?' He attempted humour. It was rejected.

'Yes, a louse. In a word.'

'Ah.'

'He behaved . . . he certainly is immature. Why should I paper it all over, pretend it never happened? If that is maturity, then . . .'

'I never once used the word!'

'No, but put your hand on your heart and swear you didn't think it.'

He had to laugh. She laughed. But hers was not the kind

of laugh that would stand up, he was thinking. The meal ended rather sooner than they expected. He was afraid she was going to cry. So was she.

This time weeks passed, and she telephoned him to ask, 'What do you think, is it really a good idea for us all to spend a cosy weekend?'

'Why not? We are all going to be seeing each other about this and that, I suppose.'

'I bow to your superior worldly wisdom.'

'Anyway, it is a very pretty place. I'm sure you'll like it.'

She laughed. At him. He joined in.

It was a pretty place. Within five minutes of each other, he from London, she from Manchester, they drove off the main road through increasingly narrow lanes, until there was a large and old building with an arch in it, leading to a courtyard, between other, scattered buildings. The 'cottage' was in fact a shabby but commodious enough house with windows on to the courtyard, and through one of them Henry and Angela were visible, sitting at a table. First Sebastian, and then, more timidly, Jody, advanced to this window past plants in tubs and a sleeping collie, and presented themselves to the couple who energetically waved and smiled and begged them to come in. As Sebastian reached the door to the kitchen, Angela ran to embrace him, kiss kiss hug hug, oh darling Sebastian, while Henry affably smiled and turned half away, and when Jody appeared, immediately afterwards, Henry went to her and held her tight. 'Sweetie,' he said and, his head bent beside hers, he whispered welcomes. Angela, beside Sebastian (their arms around each other still), observed this without turning away, and on her face appeared the fleetest shadow of loss.

Then Angela and Henry left their respective loved ones,

and began whisking plates and glasses off the table. They stood side by side, backs to the sink, smiling.

Angela was a small, pretty woman, with masses of dark curly hair, and a sprightly amused air which did not leave her as she said enthusiastically to Jody, 'I am so glad you are here. Really, it is ridiculous we haven't met long before. I kept saying so, didn't I, Henry?'

'Yes, you did, but it never seemed appropriate,' said Henry. He was a large, dark, amiable fellow, with a ruddy face, but this last was from the wine he and Angela had been drinking. Seen there, side by side, they were a pair, a match, a couple, full of well-being, full of goodwill.

'Well, thanks,' said Jody, and since Sebastian had seated himself at the table that stood in the middle of this large, shabby, pleasant country kitchen, she did too, exactly where she had observed Angela sitting, through the window. They all examined each other, not concealing it: natural enough that they should be curious, their faces, their poses, frankly said. Of course the women particularly took each other's measure, meeting for the first time: but there need be no end to the new ideas suggested by their being there in the same room. For example, remembering that Jody had more than once suggested he and Henry shared qualities, Sebastian was regarding Henry from this point of view, but concluded, behind his smile, that only an angle of vision so far from anything he could approach was capable of such a comparison, and there was no sense in even trying to achieve it. He attempted this train of thought: Angela chose Henry, and now she's chosen me, so perhaps there is something in both of us we are unaware of? But then, the parallel thought, Henry chose Angela, and then Jody, cancelled the first. Delightful Angela (perfection in every way) did not have one point where she could be matched with this dramatic Jody, who was sitting there in her elegant country clothes, her yellow hair (dyed, he supposed) shiny and smooth, smiling and open, but as it were sharpened to a fine point of intelligence behind those shrewd, observant grey eyes. A very handsome creature, this Jody. Henry was welcome to her.

'We have a problem,' announced Henry. 'Connie isn't feeling well, and we've decided to run her into the local hospital.'

'And that's why we were so rude and ate before you arrived,' confessed Angela. 'But if you'll just make your-selves at home, we'll be back in a jiffy.'

This 'jiffy' would be all afternoon, as was obvious as soon as you thought about it. Sebastian was registering Jody's look which (probably against her will) was posi-tively shouting that *surely* it must be occurring to the par-ents this indisposition of eleven-year-old Connie might be related to this traumatic occasion, the presence together for a whole weekend of her two parents and their new mates. But if the parents had this thought they were not showing it.

'She's been off-colour for some days,' said Angela. 'I nearly took her to the doctor last Saturday.'

'We'll be back in a trice,' said Henry, with a look at Jody that made her glow with pleasure, made her, suddenly, like a girl, confused and grateful. Her face, however, at once returned to its condition of sober over-alertness that was making Sebastian uncomfortable.

'Sebastian knows where everything is,' said Angela, with a special look at him.

Henry and Angela went out, and soon the other two watched them take their daughter, wrapped in a blanket and drooping between them, to a car. Off went the car under the big arch to the outside world, with smiles and waves, and even a kiss blown from Angela to Sebastian over Connie's head.

Then Sebastian got up, went to the refrigerator, and began unloading on to the table the lunch that was really only the preliminary to the big evening meal. Pâté. Cheese. Salad. Fruit. Sebastian and Jody sat together in this amiable kitchen, and, for a while, ate.

'I've never known a woman so able to make her thoughts felt,' said Sebastian, but not as if he enjoyed this quality.

'I'm certainly having plenty of them.'

He said nothing, but poured out more wine, refilling her glass without asking her.

'When, for instance, were you here last?'

'Two weekends ago. No, with Olga. And the child of course – ours. Her name is Marion. And Connie was here too for the day.'

She digested this. 'You and your former wife spend holidays together?'

'Well, yes, for the child you know. Marion has become very friendly with Connie, I am glad to say. Henry and Angela like people using this place.' Silence. He spelled out, 'We have separate bedrooms, Jody.'

'Naturally, since you are divorced.'

'Not because we are divorced, but because I love Angela.'

'Did you know that Angela and Henry were off for ten days in the spring together?'

'With Connie. They went together to visit Connie's grandmother in Switzerland – she lives there with her third husband you know. Angela's mother.' He added, 'Actually, Henry was only there a couple of days. I thought he was meeting you somewhere.'

'I thought he was too, but then he was working – in Germany.'

'Henry does work very hard. Much harder than I do.'

Henry worked in the administration of some artistic

foundation, and was always travelling. Sebastian was a businessman, and he travelled a lot too.

They ate cheese and drank more wine. Then Sebastian began to talk, choosing his words, while his manner said he felt he had to say all this, but would rather there was no necessity. 'Did you know Henry and Angela have known each other all their lives? They grew up together.'

'Yes, Henry told me.'

'Brother and sister. That's what they are like. It took me some time to see it, I admit.'

Now he looked at her, to judge if there was any need to spell it out.

She said drily, 'I'm not jealous about sex.' And added childishly, 'I've no reason to be.' Then she blushed, because of her boastfulness, again momentarily becoming a girl again.

Now he laughed at her. He was rather tipsy, and flushed, just like Henry, and relaxed and easy. As at ease as if he were in his own kitchen. 'Well, good for you,' he said. 'I, on the other hand, am capable of being terribly jealous. But not about Henry. They haven't slept together for years. They can't. It doesn't work. Sex was never the important thing, for them.'

'So Henry tells me.'

'Well, then?' He seemed antagonistic to her now, his ruddy face directed full at her, without any of his usual watchfulness and restraint. The wine had stripped that off him! Or perhaps his dislike of her had ... He was going on, 'Jealousy! If you want my advice, then don't. Don't even start. Don't let it enter things at all. I know. I've done it. And regret it.'

'With Olga?'

'Yes, and not only with Olga. With others. It is my misfortune to be jealous. And now I spend a lot of effort in not being. You can't win with jealousy, ever.'

With this warning blasted straight at her, he stood up.
'I don't think I am jealous.'

'Aren't you? That's what it looks like to me.'

But before she could say any more, he said, moving to
the door, 'I'm a bit tight. And I'm going to sleep. I don't
work half as hard as Henry does, but I like to get a bit
of a siesta when I'm here.' At the door he stopped. 'Of
course, you don't know where you are sleeping.'

'Presumably with Henry.'

'Naturally. When you get to the top of the stairs, then
go along the passage in front of you and it's at the end.'
He was almost out of the door when he turned to say,
'Angela and I are in the other direction, in case you are
wondering. Separated by at least five rooms.'

'Some cottage,' she said, but he had gone.

She sat on alone in the quiet kitchen. She could hear
Sebastian's footsteps overhead, and was pleased to hear
them. The thin English sunlight in the courtyard outside,
the way people drifted past there, a car heard passing in
the lane outside, the shadow of a bird on the stones of the
court – all this inflicted on her a mood of dispersal, change,
loss. She began to feel out of place, sitting upright, as if on
guard, her fingers around the stem of the empty wineglass.
She too should go to sleep for a while. Why not?

The bedroom at the end of the corridor was a large room,
furnished adequately for country visits, with rugs on the
floors and an old-fashioned down quilt on the vast double
bed. From the windows she looked at widely-spaced
houses in green fields. She slid into the great bed and
thought that here, tonight, she and Henry . . . well, better
wait and see.

The two came downstairs within five minutes of each
other: it was already late afternoon. Henry had rung to
say he and Angela were delayed at the hospital. Would
Sebastian and Jody start the dinner?

Sebastian, at home in this kitchen, directed operations while Jody obediently chopped and mixed, and then together they made a pudding she was good at. The courtyard outside the windows now held the last sunlight like a pool, and the plants, and the dog dozing on a flagstone, a tree, a bench, seemed remote, the setting for a song, or a story. Sebastian told Jody the history of this 'cottage' and its environs, a long one going back centuries, and full of incident, but only the last part elucidated what they were looking at. This whole area had once been a large estate, and the big archway had been where coaches, carts, teams of horses had come under the building that housed a dozen little workshops. But now a bakery, ironsmiths, the farrier's, the tannery, the carpenter's shed, the stone mason's yard, were studios for artists and students who came here all through the year on courses. These were the people, mostly young, who were slowly passing the windows like lazy fish, lingering to look up at the windy evening sky, or standing to stare at the dog, or – briefly, before manners averted their eyes – at the window where Jody and Sebastian could be seen at work. Then, as dark filled the courtyard, with the meal entrusted to the oven, the two went into the sitting room. This was, like all the house, large, shabby, and comfortable. In this room Jody's smart clothes seemed out of place, but her manner said she did not propose to apologize for them.

They had a drink. Another. Then they played Scrabble.

It was quite dark when the couple returned, entering the house with Connie still drooping between them. They shouted greetings at Sebastian and Jody, and sent apologetic smiles from the door before taking the child upstairs to bed.

Soon they were downstairs again, for it appeared that Connie was exhausted and only too ready to sleep. Angela and Henry explained how there had been delays, the doctor was always overworked . . . they took Connie to the big hospital ten miles away . . . there they had to wait again. Connie might need to have her tonsils out, but of course 'they' did not like doing the operation these days. Angela and Henry sat side by side in the ancient sofa that faced a fireplace, now empty, but it must be ever so cosy in winter. They animatedly told their story to Sebastian sitting in the large armchair on their right, and to Jody, in her armchair to their left. They turned from side to side, from one to the other, as if conscientiously allotting their attention. Then, it being dinner time, the four went into the kitchen where they ate, Henry at the head of the table, Angela at the foot. Angela was yawning, drooping, prettily apologizing: she had driven across from Switzerland this morning with Connie, after visiting her mother. She had hardly slept last night. 'Poor love,' said Henry, before Sebastian did. Angela smiled gratitude at him, and then turned her round, usually rosy, face, now drained and wan, to Sebastian, and shook her head, and smiled a helpless incapacity to do more than laugh at her own condition. Coffee was carried into the sitting room, but Angela was already asleep on the sofa. They all laughed, and this time Sebastian was in time to rouse her, and take her up the stairs to bed, supporting her as she smiled back apologies, sending kisses to everyone, including Jody who by now surely would be happy to have one.

Sebastian came down again quite soon, careful to make a noise in the hall before entering the sitting room. Henry was sitting where Angela had sat, blinking and yawning, and Jody was by him, holding his hand. She sat upright by the sprawling man, her expensively shod feet in front of her, her yellow hair gleaming.

'God,' said Henry, 'I'm so sorry, I just can't keep awake.' To Jody, 'Sorry, sweetie, I just can't . . .' And giving her a comradely hug and a kiss on her mouth, he waved at them and was off upstairs.

Sebastian and Jody did not look at each other. After coffee, they went on playing Scrabble, both running up enormous scores and claiming that the other cheated, and laughing a lot. Since they had slept so long that afternoon, it was after midnight when Sebastian joined Angela at one end of the house, and Jody joined Henry at the other. Both Angela and Henry were soundly asleep, and when Sebastian woke well after nine on Sunday morning he was alone in the room, while Jody, coming down in a housecoat, found Henry and Angela drinking coffee. It appeared they had been for a long walk. They planned to take Connie, already up and apparently quite well again, to spend the day with friends who lived not half a mile away. Would Sebastian and Jody make themselves breakfast? They did, and what Jody was not saying seemed to fill not only the kitchen, but the sitting room, when they went into it.

But back came Angela and Henry, full of animation, suggesting a good long walk: no need to bother about lunch, because they were all invited to lunch where Connie was. Off they went, the four of them, in their proper couples now, Henry and Jody in front, swinging their hands together and laughing, and Sebastian and Angela behind, with enough distance between the two pairs for love talk to be exchanged, if this were to occur. But if this did happen, it was not for long, because after a certain short halt to admire a view of high rolling hills with clouds scudding smartly across them, then Angela and Jody made the pair who came behind, a good way after the energetically striding men. That Angela and Jody should at last become friends was one of the reasons for this perilous (as Jody saw it) weekend, and what they talked about was their children. Angela was generally worried about Connie. The child had been bright and brave about the separation and then the divorce of her parents, but it had all been going on for four vital years, and while she and Henry had done everything – 'Everything we possibly could,' wailed Angela into the wind, she felt that Connie was taking it all very hard, though Henry thought she exaggerated. Here Jody told how bad she felt over Stephen, her ten-year-old. While she had remained married to Marcus, Stephen's father, she had been able to postpone the child being sent to boarding school in the English way, but with the divorce, her influence ceased. Stephen had been banished with all the heartlessness of his people to a school his father insisted on. In the holidays, she tried to have him when she could, but she worked, she held down a very good and very demanding job in the publicity department of a big firm. It was only once a year she could claim Stephen for a real holiday together. She knew the child was growing apart from her – had grown apart; she seemed increasingly exotic to him, she knew. She wanted to take Stephen to Colorado where her family ranched, for a long holiday, and she was sure Stephen wanted this, but Stephen's father claimed this would seriously unsettle an already disturbed boy. She was selfish, he said. She said he was selfish. 'We quarrel every time we meet.' But added, 'We don't actually meet, I don't want to set eyes on him again, ever. But we talk on the telephone and we always end up shouting.'

Angela listened gravely to all this, sometimes inclining her head towards Jody as the wind tugged and tore at these messages of discontent. 'Thank God Henry and I have remained good friends,' she shouted. 'At least there's not that.'

Soon they reached a pub, the goal of this walk and, it appeared, of all their country walks. A squat white building self-respectingly confronted the winds of the exposed hillside. Outside it, on a flat flagstoned area stood half a dozen white painted tables and some chairs, but these seemed about to slide away into fields and scattered gorse bushes. On this chilly day only a few people were outside, mostly those with children, exposed against a background of churning trees, rapidly moving skies, and the shimmer of the racing grasses. Inside the pub no concessions were being made to summer. A darkish room was not too well-lit with red and yellowish wall lights, and about thirty people stood or perched along the bar counter. Into this scene Henry, Angela, and Sebastian fitted themselves, as if doing it for the thousandth time, and Jody was politely welcomed. It was evident that everyone here knew these so frequent visitors from London, and in no time they were being included in the talk which, however, Jody could not follow, being gossip and information about local people, happenings and animals. This talk was loud, confident, jokey, and – from the variety of accents – included not one or two classes, but probably several: the voices of the Londoners added notes to a diapason. Not for the first time the foreigner was being made to reflect that the famous class divisions of this island were capable of easy resolution – as in this pub, for instance, where a collection of people enjoying the ritual of pre-Sunday lunch drinking in a darkish room that had something of the aspects of a cave were united by the mellow light, which, as if directed by a painter, emphasized animated faces turned towards each other, or opening in a flash of teeth to call remarks along the curve of the bar counter. It was as if some key or root definition, something primal, had only to be made and everyone here would at once agree, but these words had not been said, and never would be, for there was no need for them. In this scene was something secretive and intimate and deeply shared, something reckless and even dangerous, and Henry's face, and Sebastian's, were far from their usual humorous deprecation. As for Angela, who stood between Sebastian and Henry, she was no longer full of the woes revealed during the walk here, and her charming little face smiled often and easily at a large number of people who evidently were fond of her. No wonder this couple – a couple still – had no intention of ever relinquishing their hold on this corner of Englishness, and Jody was seeing that Sebastian was determined to be part of it too. Why, thought Jody, this is where Henry lives, where he really lives, it's not his house in London! His 'people' come from somewhere near here, but I hadn't taken that in ... He'll end up here. And I? She stood near Sebastian, between him and a large and ravaged blonde who ran riding stables: he was negotiating riding lessons for his daughter Marion. The talk went on, in a flow of its own, into news about the local hunt club and the trouble they were having with the dogs ... did Henry approve of hunting? She had never thought of asking ... there was the recent indisposition of the pub owner's pointer bitch Mabel, and the lease of fishing rights in a nearby river to some person from Japan – the amount of money being paid obviously gave everyone the maximum of satisfaction. Then the talk turned to the probable marriage of a recently widowed farmer's wife with the Belgian owner of a neighbouring farm: this earned no one's approval. It wouldn't last, it seemed everyone agreed, though the company showed a generous understanding of the sensual aspects of the affair. She was a fine armful, all right, claimed the fellow behind the counter (not mine host, the owner of the pointer bitch, but his brother-in-law). She was definitely good news, said this lean humorous character ('Foxy'), who wore a checked waistcoat that had caused him to be generally teased, a tribute he had accepted with the knowing smile and sharp rolling eye of one who knows a good thing when he sees it. No wonder this Gervais what's-his-name wanted her, he'd need his head examined if he didn't . . . but at this a certain laughter broke out around the pub: evidently he of the bright waistcoat had not been averse to this armful. He acknowledged the laughter with a judicious nod: fair enough! – but insisted, clinching the thing, that marriage needed thinking about, those two were rushing into it, no good could come of it.

Was this perhaps meant for her and Henry? – Jody was wondering, for she saw that Henry's intended marriage with an American was bound to be discussed in these forums of public opinion. Her presence here was being well-noted: and that Henry had understood was shown by his coming to stand by her, his glass in one hand, the other at her elbow. In a moment he went on with remarks apparently not addressed to anyone in particular, to the effect that he needed someone to come and mend the roof.

All this went on for a good hour or more, with people coming and going, but mostly coming: the pub was crammed. When the four left there were cries of, 'See you soon, then,' 'You'll be back? See you then!' – from all over the room. Outside they set off with the wind behind them, this time four abreast, Henry at one end holding Jody's hand, Angela at the other holding Sebastian's, but Angela and Henry were telling a story and interrupting each other with much laughter, about an incident in the village. Some imperial pumpkin had invaded one garden from the next. The invaded owner had cut off a slice from a pumpkin big enough for Cinderella's coach, on the grounds he had never tasted it, ill feeling had ensued . . . They did not go to 'the cottage' but to the house where Connie was. A small crowd of people already sat around a vast wooden table in another court, a smallish one this time, where the wind was shut out. A deep yellow sunlight filled it, pulling scent from the white roses that draped a brick wall. Connie was there, sitting with her friend Jane. Seen by daylight Connie was a tall slender child with dead black straight hair – Henry's, and black doe eyes – Angela's, both set off by the ivory cheeks of her sickness, which had apparently come on again. Jody (if not Sebastian, for he was probably used to it by now) suffered the usual shock of seeing intimately known features appropriated by a stranger. Connie and Jane were making a pair, isolating themselves against the grownups, who all recognized the need to allow Connie, allow Jane, to stare out at them with eyes full of the criticisms bred by their shared confidences, refined by the disdainful fastidiousness of their age.

Jane was the daughter of Briony who managed this estate. Briony was a strong country woman, middle-aged, with short straw-coloured hair and healthy cheeks, observant blue eyes and muscular hands gained by all the work that went with fields, woods, gardens, buildings, and their maintenance, the colony of budding artists and their supervision. It turned out that she was the divorced wife of the owner of these properties, and the mother of a son shortly to be twenty-one, Jane's elder brother by ten years or so. She had been running this place because 'poor Oliver simply doesn't have a clue, he never had, poor sweetie,' but was looking forward to relinquishing the burden the very second her son took over, when she would revert to her own true nature and inclination, which was to make stained glass windows. Jody listened to all this with more than her usual feelings of being alien. She could not begin to understand why this woman had been prepared to spend her life as a sort of caretaker for a divorced husband. Without much recompense, it seemed, for she did remark that the estate could not afford to pay her much in the way of a salary, not if there was to be anything decent for Paul (the nearly twenty-one-year-old son) to inherit.

Jody, who was sitting across the table from her hostess – soon to be, at least intermittently, a neighbour – inquired (though with the feeling that this would strike everyone as the sort of remark only to be expected from her) what she got out of it all?

Briony broke bread comfortably between the fingers of her left hand, holding her wine glass in her right, and smiled. She bestowed on Jody a regard due to the outside world (outside these islands), noblesse oblige, and said, 'This is a good place to be. I've enjoyed it. I enjoy doing it. It's rewarding.' And she sat looking through the oblong gap between grey stone buildings where the fields could be seen ascending a sharp slope to a wood, brown glistening soil already ploughed for the winter crops.

'Well,' said Jody stubbornly, facing Briony whom she very much liked, although they were so different, one so smart and shiny, one so homely and work-used, 'if it were me I'd feel I'd been made use of. You don't. Couldn't your – ex-husband have made arrangements for the estate to be run? When you leave here, what will you have to show for it all?'

Briony's nod acknowledged the justice of this. 'Well, Paul has had a very nice place to come to for his holidays. And all his friends. Jane adores it – and her friends . . .' Here she smiled affectionately at Jane, who returned an unwilling smile that acknowledged she had to admit the truth, even when bound to criticize the grownups. 'You can't have everything,' Briony summed up at last. 'I know I could have been first-class at my job – the stained glass, but I'll be good enough. And I've enjoyed everything here.'

The word enjoy had come up again.

It was an enjoyable, very long meal, with good country food, a lot of wine, and the sun pouring down into the walled place where, Briony said, the most wonderful peaches were grown every summer. Last month there had been hundreds of them. Along the wires that sectioned the walls horizontally, the peach branches stretched their now lightened branches, and a glass bowl of a rose-tinted concoction was pushed towards Jody: the peaches themselves, preserved in honey and wine.

It was nearly five when the meal ended. They were all tipsy and full of well-being, even Jody. The four went back to the cottage, leaving Connie with Jane. She had confided to her mother that she still felt a bit funny, and Angela had told her she must telephone at once if she felt any worse, when both parents would be at her bedside within five minutes.

A pity to waste what was left of the sunlight, not so dense and yellow here in the large court, but kind enough, so they sat drinking tea outside the kitchen windows. Swifts whirled and squealed about the pale blue sky. The dog, stretched out in bliss on the warm stones, flopped its tail about, when it remembered to. Bees were hard at work even after the light drained away, leaving a quiet, intimate dusk. No one said much. Of course Angela and Henry were tired, having woken so early. Once Jody made a remark that could have led to the good talk which was, she had felt, the point of this weekend, but neither Henry nor Angela took it up. She supposed she agreed with them: such an evening was too rare a thing not to be savoured minute by perfect minute.

'We aren't going to need much supper,' announced Angela, as they got up out of their chairs in the now dark court, lit patchily from an upstairs window opposite.

'No,' said Henry, 'not much, but some. I'll make my potato soup. It's quick and delicious.' He went into the kitchen, and the others were about to go into the sitting room when the telephone rang, and Angela ran to it as if she had been waiting for it. Connie announced that she felt worse. Angela called Henry who came out of the kitchen, and the two went off to their daughter. Sebastian said he was capable of making as good a soup as Henry was, and Sebastian and Jody again took on the responsibilities of the kitchen. But Jody sat herself down at the table and began to cry, making no attempt to stop. She sat there, weeping, from an old, or at least well-established well of grief, her large grey eyes wide open and the tears running, staring past Sebastian and out into the dark where now the high yellow window spilled a single shaft of light. Sebastian stood slicing potatoes and onions into a saucepan, and sometimes looked at her, when he nodded sympathetically, but continued with the task of making soup.

Her weeping made no claims on him, nor on the world. At one point he handed her a box of tissues. At another he pushed towards her a glass of wine – as if they had not already had enough of it. Later he inquired, 'Your boy?' and she nodded.

'I've lost him, you see,' she said.

He gave her a long, acute look, checking for exaggeration, and then grunted an assent. He said, 'I'm sorry, Jody. Well, it can't be easy seeing how Henry and Angela deal with it.'

With a sigh she said, 'As successful as possible, I suppose. And your child – Marion?'

'Luckily she's the same age as Connie.'

'There's your wife, not just Henry and Angela.'

He nodded. 'Right. But Olga and I have made a point of not involving poor Marion in our disagreements. I don't think we go to the lengths Henry and Angela do – to my mind they overdo it, but Marion's all right.' At

her look he insisted, 'Yes, really all right. She is doing
well at school – surely that's a pointer? She likes coming
here with Olga – they were here only a month ago, the
two of them.'

'Your ex-wife Olga, and your daughter, and Henry and
Angela and Connie and you?'

'And some other people came too. A house party. A real
one. No, I couldn't make it, I was working. I do work, you
know.'

'So do I,' she insisted. 'I work hard.'

'We all work hard. We are the hard working classes.'

She had stopped crying. She sat straight up, as was
her way, shoulders back, as if at some health course or
other she had been instructed how to sit and had never
compromised since. But her hands on the table in front
of her were clenched in the tension of her misery.

'Does your ex-husband know how you feel?' Before
she could explode at him, something he obviously felt
was imminent, he went on steadily, keeping his eyes on
her face, a kindly-meant warning, or pressure: 'I mean, I
don't think I would have known how Olga felt about it all
if we hadn't discussed it so much. And discussed it and
discussed it – ' he continued, almost frivolously, but his
laugh was rueful. 'In my view, things can be discussed
too much.'

'So I have gathered.'

'But Olga has always insisted. Everything that comes
up with Marion, everything, we talk it over. And she
was right.'

Her wide eyes again spilled tears. 'I am sure Olga
doesn't realize how lucky she is. Nor does Angela.'

'Have you actually tried to talk to him – to Marcus?'

'I think that perhaps at the beginning – but no, it's too
late now.'

'Has he married again?'

'Yes, last winter.'

'Ah.'

'Precisely. Ah. But there are such things as – situations you can't do anything about.'

'Well, I believe I am not prepared to admit to that.' This had the same note of almost frivolity which she did recognize was an attempt to lighten this tragic scene. For it was that, they both knew it.

When the outer door, and then the door into this kitchen slammed open, and Henry and Angela stood there, they were sparkling with the run across from the other house in the half dark of the lanes and paths, and then under the great arch and across this court. It was raining, they exclaimed, no, just a little, great big drops, they said. It was like a showerbath. They stood exclaiming and explaining, taking over the kitchen with their vitality.

Jody was able to go quietly out, unremarked, to dry her eyes and make up her face.

During the meal of soup and bread more wine was drunk. Angela and Henry began yawning again. They had been up since before six, they said; but Sebastian, for Jody, said that they must keep awake, because at some point this famous talk had to take place.

'Well, of course,' said Angela. 'But we'll all be here tomorrow, and it seems to me there isn't so much to discuss. Aren't we all perfectly reasonable people?'

After the meal Henry and Angela went into the sitting room, while Sebastian made the coffee. Jody stayed behind with him, and then because he said he wanted to wash up – no, she shouldn't bother – she followed the other two. When Sebastian entered the sitting room with the tray, Jody sat in the big chair opposite, chosen so the light was behind her. The other two chattered away about Briony, about Oliver, due to return from New Zealand soon, about Jane, about Jane's coming to stay with Connie in London, about a weekend next month when it would be nice if everyone could be here again.

The two sat close, turned towards each other, looking into the other's face. As one finished a remark, or suggestion, Henry, or Angela, came smartly in. Again it was impossible not to remark what a pair these two made, alike physically and in their similar country-comfortable clothes . . . and wasn't Angela wearing Henry's shirt over her trousers, sleeves turned up, making her a vulnerable little morsel against his large and reassuring roundness? Two flushed faces, alike in the mysterious way of the long married, their eyes searching each other's in a habit of picking up points where the other dropped them . . . As the talk went on, they turned still further around, were facing each other. Half an hour later, they were still at it, Grannie's possible plans for Christmas in Switzerland, Connie's need for music lessons . . .

Sebastian broke in, 'I think we should talk about how to incorporate Stephen – you know, Jody's boy. He ought to be friends with our children.'

This cut the exchange dead. Slowly Henry and Angela turned away from each other, and both leaned back and stared at Sebastian, at Jody – but her face was shadowed, as she had taken care it would be.

'Well of course,' said Henry. 'Haven't we discussed this, sweetie – surely we have?' – to Jody.

'It was mentioned.'

'Perhaps he could come here when Marion and Olga come too some time over Christmas?' This was Henry.

'A bit spartan, really, in winter, but it's lovely too.' This was Angela.

'Surely discomfort is what they are trained for,' remarked Jody. Stephen was at a famous school, not known for its comfort.

'It's a pity Stephen is a boy,' said Henry.

'Yes. If you had a girl, it would be easy. Marion and Connie get along like anything. And Jane gets on with Marion too,' said Angela.

Jody said, 'At that school they are not exactly taught how to get on with girls.' Her voice was dry, nothing of what she felt was being allowed to show. She sat with her coffee cup in her hand, the hand on the arm of the chair, a long, elegant well-kept hand. But the steady tinkle of the cup in the saucer caused Sebastian to lean forward, as if to take it from her, help her in something. Then he leaned back again, crossing his legs. She set the cup down.

'All these public schools are better than they were,' said Henry.

'Would Stephen's father allow him to join us all here for a few days?' Sebastian inquired.

'I never know what Marcus is going to allow,' said Jody. 'But if these three little girls are all such good friends, are they going to be happy with a strange boy suddenly foisted upon them?'

'We should try it,' said Angela enthusiastically.

'But we are talking as if Connie won't be at your mother's skiing,' said Henry. 'Perhaps Easter would be better?'

'When are we all going to get married?' Angela asked Henry.

'Surely you should ask Sebastian. Jody and I thought of October.'

This linking of himself with Jody startled, so much had the two not been a pair this weekend.

'October would suit me,' said Jody.

Angela said to Sebastian, 'You suggested October, didn't you? But perhaps November? There's Connie's school trip. She's going to France with her school,' she explained to the others. 'There's got to be time for dresses, that sort of thing.'

'I didn't know you were having a proper wedding,' Henry said, put out. 'If we all did something quick at the registry office, we can fit it in any time.'

'What do you mean, a proper wedding?' protested Angela. 'Not the kind *we* had, but a wedding. I want Connie and Marion to be bridesmaids.'

'Bridesmaids!' said Henry, laughing.

'Why not, they'd love it?'

'I rather doubt whether my Stephen would love Henry's and my wedding,' said Jody. 'So far he simply changes the subject.'

'How did he handle your ex ... I mean, Marcus's wedding?' asked Sebastian.

'When I asked him about it, he said it was all right,' said Jody.

Henry laughed. So did Angela. Then, soberly, for Jody's sake, Angela said, 'But it is awful. Boys are so much more difficult.'

'Particularly with that awful, ridiculous, unforgivable emotional training they get,' said Jody. Her voice was now far from cool, and Henry reached out his hand, took hers, squeezed it. The two hands dangled there, between sofa and chair, but the discomfort caused them to fall apart.

Sebastian said, 'We should discuss finance, too. I use this place with Olga. I should like to contribute.'

'We can discuss all that,' said Angela, and yawned.

'There's also the business of Connie's school fees,' said Henry to Angela. 'Did you get them paid in time?' To the others he said, 'Sorry, but we have a lot of things to discuss.'

'We haven't seen each other for – how long has it been Henry?'

'It's been weeks,' said Henry.

They had turned to face each other again. And they began again to talk about practical things, school fees, holidays, mutually convenient dates. Should Connie perhaps change schools? There must be a room for Connie in Sebastian and Angela's new flat, as well as the room for Marion. And in Henry's and Jody's flat too. And so on . . . Again it seemed as if the two were waiting for one set of words to be finished, to return another, in a close hard exchange, as if words were something tangible, an extension of the one who used them.

Throughout this weekend Sebastian and Jody had not allowed their eyes to meet in comment, but now Jody was looking steadily at Sebastian, and then he – slowly, as if determined not to evade a responsibility or an obligation – allowed his eyes to engage with hers. It was a long, sober gaze.

Again half an hour passed. Henry and Angela could not end this exchange of theirs, which continued animatedly, with exclamations, disagreements, agreements, suggestions . . . and then, a clock struck from the hall, and Angela leaped up, 'Oh goodness, I'm going to bed, I'm dropping with sleep, oh Sebastian darling, do come up soon . . .' She went out, waving at the three. But Henry followed her, and the two went up the stairs, talking hard all the way. Again the two left behind looked at each other, and went on looking, as they listened to Henry and Angela talking animatedly at the top of the stairs, until at last Henry went one way to the room he shared with Jody, and Angela the other to the room where Sebastian would shortly find her fast asleep.

A silence.

Jody said deliberately, 'They talk like that, *they have to*, because they can't make love.'

He coloured, but did not evade it. 'I have to say that this weekend I've seen things . . .'

'*Yes*,' said Jody.

'I'm going to have a drink,' he said, and it was evident

that this would enable him to turn away from her and her absolute determination he should share what she felt, and saw. Without asking her, he poured some whisky for her and put the glass into her hand. He almost did not sit down again, but then made himself: she needed so much that he should.

'I think I'm going to leave early tomorrow morning,' she said. 'I might even sleep down here tonight.'

He was certainly startled. Then, still in the same way of making an effort to meet her, said, 'Last night I don't think Angela knew I was there at all. She was worn out, poor sweet.'

'Well, yes,' said Jody, intending him to understand she took this from a quite different point of view. 'Anyway, I don't think I can stand it,' she said, tears threatening to engulf her voice. But she shook her head, took a gulp of her drink, and made herself smile.

'I know one thing, you are making a decision when you're very upset. That's always a mistake.'

'I didn't say I was making a decision, I said I was leaving . . . oh, all right, then it is a decision. But I don't think decisions made in haste are always bad ones.'

He said, 'Perhaps it is not always an advantage to be so relentlessly full of insight.' This sounded spiteful, and he added quickly, 'Oh I'm not saying you aren't right – but where does it get you? No, bear with me, I've been thinking about it – you've made me think. Am I going to be any better for seeing every little nuance . . .' Her face said satirically, *some nuance*, and he nodded impatiently. 'But perhaps I had taken a decision without knowing it *not* to see everything . . . after all, I'm going to marry Angela and we are going to be happy . . .' This tailed off, it was a bad moment: it was occurring to him (of course it had long ago to Jody, *naturally*, he was thinking angrily) that if Henry didn't marry Jody then there would be all kinds of new adjustments, complications, new balances.

'There's one thing you don't seem to see,' said she. 'Olga.'

'Olga?'

'You have Olga, *your best friend.*'

He examined this, on its merits. 'Yes, my best friend, and yes, you're right, without Olga . . . yes, without her I'd find it all . . .'

'All I have is Marcus. If you didn't have your *best friend* – has she married again, by the way?'

'No. Not yet. I am sure she would like to, but so far . . .'

'You wouldn't marry her again?'

'Look, you don't seem to . . . I love Angela. I know this weekend hasn't been . . . but I don't think you are giving it enough time. I certainly don't feel about it all the way you do.'

A pause. 'You certainly have a good time, you people.'

'Wh-a-a-at?'

She contemplated him, as he sat there with his glass in his hand. Various little scenes from the past two days came back to her, and she contemplated them, too, taking her time. Her smile, when she spoke at last, was full of condemnation. 'You are so pleased with yourselves! So – content!'

'Content? You make it sound like a crime! Well, yes, I think I am content. I like my life.' He looked at her, not long and slow, this time, only a quick glance, unable to stand the naked blaze of her unhappiness.

'I've missed out,' she said. 'That's what I've learned from you. I've missed out on the best relationship of them all. I don't have a best friend – the ex-husband, the ex-wife.' Her laugh was a squeal of misery.

He nodded, smiling, to acknowledge her wit.

'I'm sorry,' he said. He got up. 'If I were you I'd think about it. Henry's a good chap, you know. I've learned to know him well. He's all right.'

'Yes, another good friend.'

'Well,' he said, 'I don't know what to say except that . . .'

'You're sorry,' she said finally. 'And so am I.'

He went out and up to bed, and she remained sitting where she was.

By the same author

London Observed